step-, a prefix meaning related by remarriage

Why didn't they talk about what *step* really means? About how it means stepping aside so that a man who's not your father can hold your mother's hand. And how it means stepping out of the way to let a little kid scoot into the booth next to your mother so she can fold his pirate hat. And how it means stepping over a teenage girl who has taken your favorite spot on the floor and now you have to watch TV from the uncomfortable chair in the corner.

It's not that I hated the Russos. But I never put out the welcome mat and invited them into my life.

Let's face it. A welcome mat's just one more thing for someone to step on.

Other Bullseye Books you will enjoy

MY MOTHER GOT MARRIED

(and other disasters)

Barbara Park

Bullseye Books · Alfred A. Knopf
New York

To my friend and editor,

ANNE SCHWARTZ,

who smooths all the rough edges,

and lets me take all the credit

—B.P.

(one)

MY PARENTS are divorced. There's no way to make it sound nice. They're divorced, and that's that.

I live with my mother, but I'm shared with my dad. It's called joint custody. It means they both want me to know that they both want me. I stay at Dad's every other weekend and on holidays and whenever else I want to. He moved into a new apartment a few months ago. It doesn't smell as bad as his first one did.

Mom and I got to remain in the house, so at least something stayed the same. The only thing that changed was our hallway. We used to have family pictures from one end to the other. But after the divorce my mother put them away in the attic. Not all at once. Little by little, like the three of us just sort of faded off the walls.

I still go up there and look at them sometimes. She doesn't know it, but I do.

A few weeks ago my mother put a picture of Ben on the bookshelf. Ben Russo. A man who's not my father. The picture's in a silver frame. Ben's smiling. So far I haven't smiled back.

My mother met Ben last summer a few weeks after the divorce was final. She was backing our car out of the driveway when she smashed into the side of his truck. We were both wearing our seat belts, so neither one of us was hurt. Ben was planting a tree in our neighbor's front yard, so he wasn't hurt either.

When he saw the dent, he didn't jump up and down or wave his fists in the air or anything. He just put down his shovel, walked over to our car, and peered in the window.

My mother was sitting there, slumped over the steering wheel. She was saying the "s-h" word. Not loudly. Just sort of whispering it over and over again to herself.

"You hurt?" he asked her.

Mom didn't look up. She just kept muttering you-know-what.

I got out of the car. "She's okay," I assured him.

"She always does this when she crashes into something."

Suddenly my mother opened her door and got out.

"Could we please not act as though I do this every day, Charles?" she snapped, her voice sounding shaky. "I've been driving for twenty-one years and this is my first accident, okay?"

I thought it over a second. "What about last year when you ran over my bike?" I reminded her. "And then there was that light pole at Dunkin' Donuts."

My mother threw her hands in the air. *"Make a list for the man, why don't you!"* she shouted at me. *"How about telling him all the things I've sucked up in the vacuum cleaner while you're at it!"*

I don't know why Ben smiled, but he did. Then he got the name of our insurance company and went back to digging his hole. The next day he brought my mother a free tree from his plant nursery.

"Trees help calm your nerves," I heard him explain as he carried it around to the backyard to plant it.

That's all it took. One free tree and they started dating. I couldn't believe it. No chocolate, no flowers—just a dumb little tree and my mother started acting as goofy as a teenager. Every morning she'd hurry out back to water it. Then she'd sigh and say, "Wasn't that nice of him?" Seriously. She said it about a billion times.

The weird thing is that Ben Russo is just about as different from my dad as you can get. He looks like one of those nature guys. You know, the kind you see in commercials walking through the woods swinging an ax and eating acorns and wild berries. He has a beard and wears boots and a belt with a big turquoise buckle. Ben Russo would look comfortable walking around in a lumberjack shirt with a squirrel on his shoulder.

My dad is more the suit-and-tie type of man. If you put a squirrel on my father's shoulder, he'd probably run around screaming, "Get it off! Get it off!"

He tried eating a wild blackberry at my grandmother's house once. As soon as it was in his mouth he spit it out and ran inside to get a drink of water.

Ben has two kids. A teenage girl and a little boy. His wife died, so I guess he sort of got stuck raising them by himself. I know it sounds sad, but that doesn't mean I automatically have to like him.

I don't exactly understand what my mother sees in him anyway. Ben hardly ever talks and when he does, it's usually real soft and quiet.

What's so exciting about hanging around a dull guy like that?

It's hard, you know? Watching your own mother start to like a man who's not your father. A guy who sells trees instead of insurance. A man who doesn't know your birthday or your middle name or where your room is. It sort of makes you queasy, if you want to know the truth.

Besides, I just always thought I'd be all the family my mom would ever need. Even with Dad gone, the two of us still had a good time together.

Like sometimes on Saturday mornings we'd go to the World of Waffles and she'd let me order the kind with strawberries and whipped cream. When we first started going, I was a little self-conscious. I kept thinking people were staring at me, wondering why there wasn't a dad with us. But after a while it didn't bother me anymore.

We went to movies together, too. We'd get popcorn or Dots or Junior Mints. Just the two of us. It was fun.

At least I thought it was.

WHENEVER something bothers me, I'm supposed to talk it over with my parents. That's the advice my psychologist, Dr. Girard, gave me. "Problems never get solved by keeping your feelings all bottled up inside you," he said.

I met Dr. Girard last year when we were going through the divorce. I'm not really embarrassed about it. Dr. Girard was a pretty cool guy to talk to. Besides, I wasn't crazy or anything. It's just that some kids don't stay as calm during a crisis as others. Like if I was ever cornered in my basement by a vampire, I wouldn't be in control enough to make a cross out of two paint sticks or shine a mirror in his eyes. I'd be too busy running around screaming.

I haven't seen Dr. Girard lately, but I still try to remember some of the stuff he told me. That's why I finally decided to talk to my mother about Ben. Sometimes if you don't talk, the pressure builds up and you can explode all over the place. Not your insides. Your emotions.

I waited until she and Ben had had four dates before I said anything. Two movies and two dinners. Until then, I'd just been trying to put up with it. It wasn't working, though. Seeing them go out together made my stomach feel funny.

Finally I just couldn't stand it anymore. On their fourth date I stayed awake until Ben brought her home. Then I went to the top of the stairs and listened for his truck to drive away.

I waited patiently while Mom paid Paul Hall for staying with me. Paul's this high school kid who lives next door. He gets paid, but he's not a baby-sitter. Baby-sitters take care of you. Paul Hall just slumps in our recliner and watches the Movie Channel.

After he left, my mother turned on the news. As quick as a flash, I was standing in the doorway clearing my throat. I already knew what I was going to say. I'd been thinking about it all night.

"I don't want you to go out with him anymore," I announced simply. "He's not Dad and it makes me queasy."

My mother jumped a foot. She scares easier than she used to.

I sat down on the couch and continued. "He doesn't fit in with us like Dad did. He's too different."

Mom raised her eyebrows. "Different?"

I nodded. "Just look at him. He's nothing like Dad. He probably goes out to the forest every morning and eats a bowl of fiber cereal."

I'm not sure how long my mother stood there staring. But finally she turned off the news and moved onto the couch next to me. Her expression had turned to puzzlement.

"You don't like Ben? Is that what you're saying?"

I shrugged. Liking him had nothing to do with it. I just didn't want him, that's all. We didn't need him.

"I don't understand this at all, Charlie," Mom continued. "Ben and I hardly know each other. We're just friends. There's no reason for you to feel so strongly about him."

I rolled my eyes. Who did she think she was kidding? Just friends? Ha! Another lie! Another big fat lie!

Parents lie all the time. It comes so easily to them, they hardly even know when they're doing it. They start you off with the one about the tooth fairy and go from there.

"Put your tooth under your pillow," they'll say when you're too young to know any better. "After you're asleep, a little fairy will buzz into your room, sneak it out from under you, and leave money."

A fairy. Yeah, right. Tell me another one.

And how about all those food fibs they tell you when they want you to eat your dinner? Like "Carrots help you see in the dark" or "Bread crusts make your hair curly."

I'm not kidding. My parents said junk like that so much, I used to think I'd end up with bushy hair and x-ray vision.

Let's face it, parents don't exactly build a lot of trust by fibbing all the time. So when my mother sat on the couch that night and told me that she and Ben Russo were just friends, it's no wonder I didn't believe her.

"The two of you were holding hands when you left tonight," I informed her cleverly. "That is not being friends. That's being something else."

She frowned. "Sometimes friends hold hands."

I shook my head. "No, they don't. Not after you get out of preschool. Martin Oates is my best friend and I've never held his hand once. Not even when crossing a busy street."

Mom paused a second and gave me a funny look. "Wait a minute. How did you see us holding hands, anyway? You weren't on the roof spying again, were you?"

Geez, why can't she ever get this straight? Just because a guy likes to sit up on the roof and be alone sometimes doesn't mean he's spying.

"I've told you a hundred times, I don't spy," I explained. "I just happened to be climbing around up there and you just happened to be down on the ground holding hands and I just happened to see you."

My mother made sort of a hissing sound. She's never been very understanding about the time I spend on the roof. Ever since I spotted her dancing with our neighbor's dog in the back yard, she's been pretty unreasonable about it.

"Remember Santa Claus, Charlie?" she asked then. "Remember the year you thought he was spying on you from the North Pole with high-powered binoculars?"

I felt my face getting red. Why did she have to bring that up again?

"It wasn't my fault," I explained for the millionth time. "It was the stupid song. The one about how he knows when you're sleeping and when you're awake and if you've been bad or good. Doesn't that sound like spying to you?"

Mom wasn't listening. "Remember how you kept turning toward the North Pole and waving? And how you spent the entire week before Christmas searching the house for hidden microphones? You thought the star on top of our tree was taking pictures."

"It blinked funny," I muttered quietly.

"Well, you didn't like it *then*, and I don't like it *now*. I'm an adult, Charles. And I deserve to have friends, just like you do. And I ought to be able to go out once in a while and get in someone's car without wondering if my son is up on the roof doing a routine stakeout."

She was making me sound ridiculous. Like a little secret agent or something. I circled my arms around my knees and hid my head.

For the next minute or two, both of us sat

there not saying a word. Then finally Mom drew a deep breath and let her cheeks fill up with air. She let it out slowly. When it was all gone, she seemed a little calmer.

"Look," she said softly. "We've both had a tough year and things still haven't completely settled down yet. But friends can help. You have yours and I have mine. And I hope that both of us keep making new ones."

I wanted to mention that none of mine would be holding my hand, but I didn't.

"Ben and I have had four dates. Four dates as friends. He's a nice man. And I like him. But most of the time he's busy with his own kids and his business. And there's simply no need for you to worry about whether he fits in here or what kind of cereal he eats."

She tousled my hair. "Come on. What d'you say?"

I looked up. What could I say? My whole argument had turned out stupid.

I shrugged my shoulders.

After that we hugged for a minute, then I went upstairs. I can't really say I felt much better. But I didn't feel any worse either. At least now my feelings were out in the open. At least now I wouldn't explode.

Not for a while, anyway.

(two)

IT WAS nine o'clock on Saturday morning. I had just gotten up. I'd been awake since eight, but when you're eleven, it's not really cool to bail out early and watch *The Smurfs*. Not even if you still want to.

When I finally made it down to the kitchen, my mother was already outside hanging sheets on the clothesline. We have a dryer but she says that sheets smell fresher if they're hung outside. It also makes them stiff as a board.

I was just about to pour some milk on my bowl of cereal when I heard a truck pull up in the driveway. I couldn't see it, but I looked out the window and saw my mother fluffing her hair, so I figured it must be Ben. A second later, she dropped the clothespins out of her mouth and ran around to the front of the house to greet him.

I wondered why he was here. To plant another tree, maybe? Or spread some fertilizer? But that wouldn't make sense. He'd already done those things the week before.

I put down the milk. If I wanted to know what Ben Russo was up to, I'd simply have to interrupt my breakfast and sneak a peek at him through the dining room window.

I was just heading into the hallway when I heard the front door slam. It was them! My mother was bringing Ben inside and I wasn't even dressed yet! I still had on my Superman pajamas! The old, faded ones that say MAN OF STEEL across the front.

I have a rule. No one except my family gets to see me in my Man of Steel pajamas. I made the rule last year after I accidentally wore them into the kitchen one Saturday morning and found this strange guy fixing the drain. His name was stitched across his shirt pocket. MAURICE. He was from France.

"Hey, Superman," he said when he saw my pj's (only with his French accent, it sounded more like "Supairman"). "Eef you've got some free time, 'ow about looking tru teese pipes and finding hair clogs for me." Then he roared for about fifteen minutes. He roared in English.

That's when I made my pajama rule. Until someone makes a dignified pair of pajamas for kids my age, no one outside the family will ever get a chance to laugh at me again.

Their voices were getting louder and louder. Oh geez, they were coming into the kitchen! I had to hide! There was no time to lose!

Quickly I shoved the milk back into the refrigerator and grabbed the box of Fruity Flakes. I learned this from watching TV. It's called removing the evidence. If I could make it to the broom closet, they would never even suspect I was up yet.

Hurry! Hurry! I screamed silently. They're almost here! Quick! My heart was pounding like crazy as I lunged for the closet door.

I made it! Just in the nick of time I was able to wedge myself in between the sponge mops and pull the door closed behind me. My foot was in the bucket, but if no one noticed my fingertips holding the door shut, I would be safe.

They entered the kitchen talking and laughing. Ben and my mother and . . . wait a second. There were other voices too. The two of them weren't alone.

"Hey! What's that?" asked a small voice. It

sounded like Beaver Cleaver. But that was impossible. Beaver Cleaver was just a TV character. And besides, he usually hung around with Larry Mondello on Saturdays.

Suddenly I felt a slight tug on the broom closet door. It caught me by surprise. I tightened my grip and tried to hold on. Outside the door I felt someone touch each of my fingers. One by one—like they were being counted.

"What are you doing over there, Thomas?" I heard Ben ask.

Whoever Thomas was, he didn't answer. Instead, he got a better grasp on the door handle and yanked with all his might. I lost my hold. And the door came swinging wide open.

A small boy stood in front of the open closet door and stared at me in wonder. His face was covered with freckles and his ears stuck out. Also, his mouth was agape. Agape means "hanging open."

His wasn't the only one, either. My mother's mouth and Ben's mouth were agape too. So was the mouth of the teenage girl standing next to them.

I'm not sure how long we stood there like that. All I know is that the boy was in serious danger of drooling, when the pressure of all that silence finally got to me.

"Boo," I muttered stupidly.

My mother's eyes widened. "Charles?" she asked, as if she had been hoping it wasn't really me.

I forced an embarrassed grin. Yup, it was me all right. It was Charles. Charles W. Hickle—Man of Steel.

Mom raised her eyebrows. "Er . . . exactly what are you doing in the closet?"

Dying, I wanted to say. Can't you see I'm dying? But instead I looked around and shrugged. "Nothin'."

Ben looked worried. "Charlie," he said calmly and slowly. It was the kind of voice that doctors use in the movies when they talk to insane people in a mental ward. "I'd, uh, like you to meet my children. This is Lydia, and that's my son, Thomas."

Cautiously Lydia raised her hand and waved a few of her fingers.

I waved my box of Fruity Flakes. It's all I could think of.

"Hey, Dad, look!" exclaimed Thomas, pointing excitedly. "He's got jammies just like mine!"

I tried to cover up, but Lydia had already started to laugh.

At last it finally dawned on my mother why I was there.

"Ohhhh," she said as the light bulb went off in her head. "I get it. You're not dressed yet, are you?"

Good, Mom. Very good.

"Listen," she said, turning to the others. "Why don't the four of us go outside and unload the plants you brought over. That'll give Charles a chance to run upstairs and get his clothes on."

Then, without waiting for an answer, she ushered Ben and his kids outside.

I have never been so humiliated in my entire life. I'm serious. Even the time I was singing in the school chorus and a big wad of underwear was hanging out of my zipper, it wasn't as bad as this.

I checked the kitchen carefully before making a mad dash for my room. When I finally got there, I shut the door, changed into jeans and a sweatshirt, and threw myself on the bed.

Why in the world had Ben brought his stupid kids over anyway? Didn't they have anything better to do on a Saturday morning? Hadn't they ever heard of TV?

And why didn't my mother warn me they were out there? Was that too much to ask? A little warning that there were strangers lurking around? Hadn't I explained the pajama situation to her after the problem with Maurice? What did

I have to do? Sleep in my clothes? Or maybe I should just lock myself in my room and never come out. That'd teach her. I could do it, too. All I needed was something to block the door, a little food, and a porta-potty.

I hadn't been brooding very long when a quiet knock on my door interrupted my thoughts.

"Dressed yet, Charlie? Can I come in?"

I couldn't believe it! She was actually at my door! What was wrong? Hadn't she humiliated me enough?

I buried my head in my pillow. "No!" I answered. "No to the first question. No to the second question. The answers are no and no."

Ignoring me, my mother took a quick peek into my room. She does this sort of thing all the time. Like a quick peek is not an invasion of privacy.

When she saw I was dressed, she opened it all the way and hurried in. Thomas was beside her. He was covering his face with his hands and peeking through the cracks. Don't ask me why, but I think he was hiding.

"Hi," she said cheerfully, pretending that nothing was wrong. "Guess who I brought with me?"

I rolled my eyes. Gee. This was going to be a tough one.

"It's Thomas!" she announced. And as she did he uncovered his face.

Golly. What d'ya know. It was Thomas.

"Thomas wanted to know if he could see your room," she explained. "So I told him, 'Why, sure you can, Thomas. Charlie would love to show you his room.'"

I frowned.

"*Wouldn't* you, Charlie," she added, more sternly this time.

Then she stood across from me and silently mouthed, "Come on. He's only five." I was still trying to figure out what his age had to do with anything when she made a break for the door.

"The rest of us will be in the back yard. Holler if you need us," she called, hurrying down the stairs.

I couldn't believe she'd done this to me! Sticking me with Thomas, of all people! The kid who exposed my pajamas to the world! What was I supposed to do with him, anyway?

He was standing in the middle of the room rocking back and forth on his heels. I looked at him, but I didn't speak. He didn't seem to mind. He just kept rocking back and forth, quietly looking the place over. Then, when he was finished, he walked calmly over to my desk, held out his finger, and started touching stuff.

He began with my pencils. Carefully he touched each of them, one by one, on their erasers. Then he moved on to my digital clock, my scissors, my high-intensity lamp, and some baseball cards that were scattered across my desktop. When he got to my globe, he held it up in the air and spun it around.

"Can I have this?" he asked nicely.

I shook my head no. He put down the globe and headed for the closet. On the way he touched three race cars on my wallpaper—a red one, a blue one, and a green one. I'm not kidding. It was spooky.

Once he disappeared into the closet, I figured that was the end of him. It's really a mess in there. My friend Martin Oates thinks there's a hand living underneath my clothes pile. He says that someday it will reach out and grab my ankles, and no one will ever see me again.

I wondered if I should mention it to Thomas. But after only a few seconds he popped out on his own. He was holding his nose.

Next he moved his touching tour to my dresser. I have a couple of stuffed animals up there, and he tried to squeak their noses. When nothing happened, he picked them up and squeezed harder. You could tell he was getting frustrated. Finally I said, "They don't squeak," and he put them back.

This whole thing took about ten minutes. When he had finished, he walked over to the window screen and hollered, *"I'm done!"* Then he sat down in my chair and patiently waited for someone to come get him.

It was Ben. I heard his boots coming up the stairs. It made me feel funny. My mother must have told him where my room was. I wondered if she had told him my middle name was Walter.

The door was wide open, but Ben knocked on the door frame. Thomas ran to him and held up his arms. He was too big to be picked up, but Ben picked him up anyway. He dangled there for a second and his dad put him down again.

Ben smiled self-consciously.

"Sorry we caught you off guard this morning."

I would have said, "That's okay," but I didn't want to lie.

After a second he turned to Thomas. "Well, can you thank Charlie for watching you?"

Thomas frowned. "He didn't watch me. I watched my own self."

Ben took Thomas's hand, but he didn't leave. I could tell by the look on his face that there was something else on his mind. Something more important than just taking Thomas back downstairs.

It made me uncomfortable. I started to squirm. It was awkward having Ben in my room without my mother along. Until then, the two of us hadn't really had a conversation. Mostly we'd just said hi, see you later, and how'd you like the movie.

"Uh . . . Charlie," he began at last. "Your mother and I were talking, and we thought that maybe next Saturday morning we could all go out for breakfast together. You know . . . the five of us."

I wiggled around restlessly on the bed. Don't say "the five of us," I thought. There are two of *us* and three of *you*, but that doesn't add up to "the five of us."

Ben cleared his throat and forced another awkward smile.

"It's just that . . . uh, we thought that it was time for all of us to get to know each other better."

Suddenly I felt sick. I bent my head and nervously started picking lint off my bedspread. I couldn't look up. I just couldn't.

He paused a second. "Um, well . . . what d'you say?"

I knew I should answer. But I couldn't. The

words he had just used kept echoing around in my head.

It's time for all of us to get to know each other. It's time. . . .

I guess it was pretty clear from my reaction that I didn't want to go to breakfast—or anyplace else for that matter.

Finally Ben mumbled, "Think it over," and left the room.

On the way out, Thomas touched all the knobs on my dresser drawers.

(three)

WE WENT to breakfast. Ben picked us up. When I got in the back seat I was very nervous. Lydia said hi. I waved. Sometimes when I'm tense, I act like a nerd.

I hadn't really paid much attention to Lydia before, but she was sitting on the very edge of the seat, so I had the chance to study her. She had the same freckles as Thomas, but her hair was too long to tell if her ears stuck out.

I wondered if they both looked like their mom. My mother told me that Mrs. Russo had died when Thomas was just a baby. I didn't know a lot of the details, but still it got to me. Having your mom die must be just about the hardest thing in the world. Harder than divorce, even.

Lydia seemed pretty normal, though. "How far away is this restaurant, anyway?" she asked as soon as we pulled out of the driveway. "I told Emily I'd be at her house at ten thirty and if we don't eat fast I'm going to be totally late."

"I'm not gonna eat fast," Thomas stated loudly. "I'm gonna eat really slow. Right, Dad? Eating slow is better for you, right?"

Lydia looked at Thomas and stuck out her tongue. I didn't want to, but it made me smile. You don't usually think of girls her age still doing stuff like that.

Thomas sat between the two of us. I tried to ignore him, but he kept staring at me like I was a freak. Halfway there, he reached out and touched me with his pointer finger.

It seemed like forever before Ben finally pulled the car into the restaurant parking lot.

"Oh, boy, World of Waffles!" squealed my mother, sounding like a little kid. "Charlie loves it here, don't you, Charlie?"

I mumbled, "It's okay," and hurried out of the car. The sooner we got this over with, the better.

The hostess spotted me coming through the door and grabbed a handful of menus.

"Good morning, sir," she said cheerfully,

knowing perfectly well that I wasn't a sir yet. "How many in your party this morning?"

"This isn't a party," I informed her bluntly.

Mom held up five fingers. "Five! We're five!" she shouted so loudly that the entire restaurant turned around to stare.

"Hey!" blared Thomas. "Guess what? I'm five, too!"

Lydia stared down at him. "We're all thrilled for you, Thomas," she said dryly.

Finally the hostess led us to a large booth in the corner. Mom slid in first. Then Lydia. I was planning to sit on my mother's other side, but Thomas beat me to it.

"Beep-beep! Beep-beep!" he honked as he plowed through Ben and me to get into the booth.

"Thomas!" said Ben. But that's all he did about it. He didn't take him out in the parking lot and punch him or anything.

The waitress brought a booster seat. As soon as Thomas climbed in, he started measuring how high his head was.

"Hey! Look how tall I am. I'm the biggest one at the table!"

Then he tapped me on the shoulder. "Hello, shorty," he said.

The kiddie menu could be folded into a pirate

hat. Thomas handed it to my mother and she fixed it for him. He put it on his head.

"Aye-aye, matey!" he sang out.

Embarrassed, Lydia slumped down in the seat. "Could someone *puhleez* do something about him?" she begged.

No one did, though, and things didn't get any better. Thomas and I both ordered waffles with whipped cream and strawberries. As soon as mine came he reached out with his finger and stole a big gob of whipped cream off the top of mine.

"Hey! Knock it off!" I blurted. "You've got your own!"

My mother turned her head and looked at me. Then she shook her head—like I shouldn't have yelled at him; like having some germy little mitt in your whipped cream was a privilege or something.

Fortunately Ben came to my rescue. "Keep your hands to yourself, Thomas," he said sternly.

After I was finished, I excused myself and waited outside on the curb. I know it wasn't polite just to leave like that, but Thomas was playing with the food on his plate and it was making me sick.

As usual, on the way home all anyone talked about was how stuffed they were. Anytime you go to a restaurant, the conversation on the way home is always the same.

"I ate too much," said Ben predictably.

"Me too," said my mother. "One more bite and I would have burst."

Just then Thomas made a loud exploding noise. "I did! I bursted! Did you hear me?"

As soon as we pulled into my driveway I opened the car door. We were still moving, but I didn't care.

"Thanks for the breakfast, Mr. Russo," I mumbled. I didn't mean it, but whenever I don't mumble thank you, I get a lecture.

I hurried up the sidewalk. The front door was locked, so I sat on the step and watched as my mother said her good-byes.

A few minutes later she came waltzing up the walk. "That was nice," she chirped. "Wasn't that nice? That was really nice."

In the next hour or two she must have said how nice it was a million times. Usually when you say a million, it means you're exaggerating. But I'm not. I swear it was a million.

Every time she said it I felt sicker and sicker. I couldn't believe this was happening. Just when my life had finally started to settle down, my stupid mother had to mess things up all over again! I know you're not supposed to call your mother stupid, but it's how I felt.

We did a lot more stuff with the Russos after that first breakfast. Picnics, a few movies and barbecues, junk like that. And even though I got to know them better—and Thomas finally stopped touching me—every time we were together the sick feeling came right back.

Just like with the divorce, I was being swept along to places that I didn't want to go. And even though my mother promised—*promised*—that she wouldn't make any decision about Ben without talking to me first, I was beginning to get nervous. Very, very nervous.

SEVEN months. That's how long it took before the announcement finally came. It was a Saturday night in February. My mother had made a big pot of spaghetti and asked Ben and Thomas and Lydia over to eat with us. After they said they'd come, she asked me if it was okay. I just shrugged. Why did she always ask *after* they were already invited?

We sat down to eat at six. Since spaghetti is my favorite meal, I was the first one finished. Thomas was last. Spaghetti takes longer to eat when you suck up each noodle like a vacuum cleaner.

Lydia shook her head. "You're such a toad,

Thomas," she told him. Then she looked at me. "He's a toad. Am I right?"

Happily I nodded.

"Use your napkin, Thomas," Lydia commanded then. "Come on, you've got sauce all over your face. Daaaad, do something. He's so gross."

Ben hardly seemed to be listening at all. He just kept fidgeting with his napkin and drinking a lot of water.

Finally, when I was just about to leave the table, he cleared his throat like he had something to say. It surprised me. Normally Ben isn't much of a talker. Ben's more a listener and a nodder.

He stood up. His face was slightly red. He seemed embarrassed and excited and nervous all at the same time. "Er . . . Janet? Could you come over here a second?"

Mom had started clearing the dishes. She put down the plates and joined him at the head of the table.

Ben smiled sheepishly. Then he reached into his shirt pocket and pulled something out.

"It's just that . . . well, I thought it would be nice if we were all here when I put this on your finger, that's all," he said softly. "All right?"

He held it up for us to see. It was a ring. A gold ring with a small sparkly diamond.

Gently Ben took my mother's left hand and slipped the ring onto her fourth finger. Her engagement one.

Mom sort of gasped. You could tell she hadn't been expecting it. I guess most people don't get engaged while they're scraping food into the sink. Then her face lit up and she looked at me and at Lydia and at Thomas. And then she hugged Ben so hard I thought I heard a little whoosh of air go out of him.

"Oh wow!" screeched Lydia, making this tiny high-pitched squeal that only girls and dolphins can make. "Oh, Janet, let me see! Let me see!"

Thomas wasn't as excited as his sister. When my mother and Ben hugged, he wrinkled up his nose and said, "Mushy." Then he looked back at his plate and tried to score a goal with his meatball.

It rolled onto the floor and landed near my foot. I picked it up, put it in the sink, and quietly left the room.

I went upstairs and called my father.

"Come get me" was all I said.

I walked outside and waited on the porch. First I sat, then I stood, then I started pacing up and down. I didn't cry, though. It surprised me, but I didn't.

By the time my mother spotted me, I was

shivering like crazy. She brought me my jacket. As she helped me with the sleeves she stopped and gave me a long, warm hug.

"I'm really sorry, honey. Ben's sorry, too," she said gently. "He didn't know about the promise."

I shrugged. It seemed shrugging was becoming my major method of communication lately.

"Dad coming?"

I nodded.

She held me a minute longer. "We'll talk when you get home."

Just then my father pulled into the driveway. He and Mom waved. They didn't end up as best friends, but at least they've been able to maintain a waving relationship.

We drove to the apartment in silence. I know it was hard for Dad not to bombard me with a million questions. Unlike Ben, my father is not a nodder and a listener. My father is an insurance salesman.

As soon as we got there he pulled out the sleeper sofa and got some pillows. It was only seven thirty, but if you're acting weird, parents like to put you to bed anyway. I gave him a funny look.

"You don't have to go to sleep. Just thought you might want to get comfortable while you're watching TV," he explained.

I plopped down and covered my head with a pillow. Then Dad brought out some popcorn and turned on the television. I stared blankly at the screen. I still don't know what was on that night.

Finally he just couldn't stand it anymore. He turned down the volume on the set.

"Is this about Ben? Did something happen over there tonight?"

I took a deep breath and nodded. There was no sense keeping it inside. It didn't feel good in there.

"They're going to get married," I managed. "They told us tonight at dinner. Ben pulled out a ring and put it on Mom's finger and—"

I stopped for a second. The lump in my throat made it hurt to talk. My eyes started filling up with tears.

"Geez, Dad. Why couldn't they just stay friends? What's so great about Ben Russo anyway?"

I looked up. My father had an odd expression on his face. Like he had just had the wind knocked out of him or something. It took me a second to realize that he was almost as upset by the news as I was. I guess it's weird finding out that your wife is marrying another man. Even if she's not your wife anymore.

He sat there a minute staring down at the floor. Like he was trying to sort out his feelings. It gave me hope. It shouldn't have, but it did.

"Maybe it's not too late, Dad," I blurted out suddenly. "Maybe you and Mom could still . . ."

But my father didn't let me get any further. He shook his head. "No, Charlie," he said firmly. "That's over and done with. You know that."

Then he took a deep breath. "I'm afraid this is one of those things you're just going to have to accept."

It made me mad, the way he said it. Like having a whole new family move into my life was just a minor inconvenience that I'd have to get used to, like a chipped tooth or a bad haircut.

I threw my hands in the air. "Sure, Dad. No problem. Just one more little adjustment in my life, right? First I start out with two parents. Then all of a sudden they get divorced and I lose my father. Then my mother backs into some guy's truck and what d'ya know, I've got a dad again. Only this one comes with a teenage sister who calls my mother Janet and a goofball little brother. And what d'ya know, all I have to do is accept it. Hey, that sounds easy enough."

Dad looked hurt. "I've never stopped being your father, Charlie. Not for one minute. Don't put that on me. It's not fair."

I turned away from him and covered my face with my hands. "Tell me about fair, Dad. It seems like nothing in my whole life is fair anymore."

He didn't answer. There was nothing more to say. Not even for an insurance salesman.

STEP—A DEFINITION

Sometimes I look up words in the dictionary. *Divorce, psychology*—words that affect my life, you know? And I wonder how they do it. The people who write the dictionaries, I mean. How do they take complicated stuff like divorce and psychology and make them sound so simple?

I looked up *step*. Not the kind of step like in a stair step or putting one foot in front of the other. I looked up the kind of step you get when your mother remarries. Like when you get a stepfather or stepbrother or stepsister. And the dictionary said: **step-** , a prefix meaning related by remarriage.

And I wondered how the dictionary could make it all sound so easy.

Why didn't they talk about what *step* really means? About how it means stepping aside so that a man who's not your father can hold your mother's hand. And how it means stepping out of the way to let a little kid scoot into the booth next to your mother so she can fold his pirate hat. And how it means stepping over a teenage girl who has taken your favorite spot on the floor and now you have to watch TV from the uncomfortable chair in the corner.

It's not that I hated the Russos. In another situation, even Thomas might have grown on me. But I never put out the welcome mat and invited them into my life.

Let's face it. A welcome mat's just one more thing for someone to step on.

(four)

IN THE weeks before the wedding, my mother tried hard to be extra nice to me. Parents do this sort of thing when they feel guilty about something.

One week we went to the movies three times. Each time I got to have a box of Dots plus Junior Mints, plus popcorn, plus a soda. If that's not guilt, what is?

One Sunday afternoon she packed a couple of sandwiches in a backpack and we went to the park to eat them. We sat under my favorite tree. The one with branches so low, it practically begs to be climbed.

"I love you, Charlie," she said out of the clear

blue as she handed over an egg salad sandwich. She'd been saying stuff like that a lot lately.

"The important things will never change between us. You know that, don't you?"

I shrugged. "Yeah, sure. Whatever you say," I answered weakly.

Mom stopped rummaging through the backpack and sighed.

"I wish you wouldn't keep acting like this."

"Like what? I'm not acting like anything," I argued.

She took me by the shoulders. "You're acting like you don't believe me. I've told you at least a hundred times that nothing is ever going to come between you and me, and I mean it. Not Ben, not Lydia, not Thomas . . . not nothin' or nobody, no how, no way."

She laughed and she reached over and tousled my hair. "Got that?"

I couldn't help but smile a little. "Yeah . . . I got that."

We hugged. It was sort of nice.

THERE WERE only about twenty people at the wedding. My mother wore a suit. I didn't know women were allowed to wear suits to weddings, but I guess it's legal.

The ceremony only took fifteen minutes. Mom

and Ben repeated the usual junk and the minister told Ben to kiss the bride. Then my mother puckered up right there in public and everybody started clapping. Everybody but me. I only clap when I like something.

Afterward, there was a reception at a nearby restaurant. They had a band and everything. Thomas asked me to dance.

"Shh!" I said, checking to make sure no one had heard. "Boys don't dance with boys, Thomas."

Thomas frowned. "We're not boys anymore, Charrulls. We're *brothers*," he declared. Then he circled his fork over my plate like an airplane and stabbed my last bite of wedding cake. The one with all the icing.

I shoved my chair away from the table and stood up. I'd get another piece of cake. Only this time I'd sit in the men's room and eat it by myself.

Suddenly I felt someone grab my arm. I turned around. It was Aunt Harriet. The one who's married to Uncle Bunkie. The Aunt Harriet who weighs two hundred pounds.

"Come on, kiddo. Polka with your old aunt."

My eyes opened wide in fear. No, God, *please*, I thought. Please don't make me do this. Please make Aunt Harriet disappear. Zap her or something. But God must have left town right after the wedding. Because the next thing I knew, the two of us were running all over the dance floor. That's what the polka is—running all around the room while some guy named Fritz plays the accordion. We didn't stop until Aunt Harriet started getting sweaty.

After the reception, my mom and Ben drove to New England for a weekend honeymoon. Thomas begged to go with them, but my mother said that taking children on your honeymoon was something only the Brady Bunch would do.

I stayed at Dad's. I didn't see Mom and Ben again until Monday morning, when my father dropped me off at the house before school. As I headed down the hall to the kitchen I could hear the two of them eating breakfast.

When I walked in, Ben was wearing a plaid robe and slippers. He was sitting in my dad's chair.

As soon as he saw me he put down his coffee cup. "Charlie," he said, smiling warmly. I'm not sure if I smiled back. I don't think so.

My mother ran to greet me with a hug. I think I was supposed to say "Welcome home," but I couldn't take my eyes off of Ben.

"Miss me?" Mom asked, squeezing me tightly.

Meanwhile, Ben reached back to the counter

and grabbed a paper bag. "We brought you something," he added eagerly.

I took the bag and looked inside. It was a paperweight shaped like Plymouth Rock.

"It's a paperweight shaped like Plymouth Rock," he said.

I stared at it a minute, turning it over and over in my hands. "Oh," I muttered.

SCHOOL WAS a waste that day. I couldn't concentrate at all. During science Mrs. Berkie strolled over to my desk and pretended to knock on my head. "Anyone home?" she said jokingly.

Yeah, I thought. And he's wearing a plaid robe and sitting in my father's chair.

After school his pickup truck was in the driveway. It was filled with stuff. Their stuff. Mattresses, a grandfather clock, a big white desk. Furniture that would look like strangers in our house.

I guess I should have been glad they were moving into our house instead of the other way around. After all, our house was bigger, and at least I got to stay in my own room. But unfortunately there was one small problem. And it was a problem I hadn't counted on.

"You understand that you and Thomas will have to share your room for a while," my mother told me at lunch one day. "You knew that, right?"

The fork dropped straight out of my mouth. "No!" I yelled. "No! Not my room. It's not fair. My room is the only thing I'm going to have left. They're the brother and sister! Make them share a bedroom."

My mother's expression turned angry. "Thank you, Charles, for your wonderful generosity. Thank you for making this so easy for all of us."

"You're welcome," I said, right out loud.

"Lydia is a girl," she said then, as if this were something I didn't already know. "You and Thomas are boys."

"Lydia and Thomas are Russos," I retorted. "I am a Hickle." Clever stuff like that comes to me sometimes.

My mother took a couple of deep breaths. I think she was trying to control her voice so MaryAnn Brady, our busybody next-door neighbor, couldn't hear her yelling.

Mom put her hands on my shoulders. "Here's the deal," she informed me matter-of-factly. "When Thomas moves in, the two of you will share a room. Your room. But as soon as Ben and I are able, we will have an extra bedroom built onto the back of the house. And if you want, you can have first choice: Either the new room or your old room."

She removed her hands and started to walk away. "I'm sorry, but that's as fair as I can be right now. You'll just have to accept it."

Accept it. Gee. What d'ya know.

I'LL NEVER forget watching them move in. Ben and a friend of his from the plant nursery carried Thomas's bed up the stairs and set it down in the middle in my room.

"Where should we put it, Charlie?" Ben asked me.

Put it back where it came from, I wanted to say. Back in your old house. But instead I pretended not to hear him and went downstairs.

Later, when I came back, everything was changed. Thomas's bed was jammed in the corner by the window. A white chest with red knobs was shoved up next to it. A baby's chest. That's what it looked like. The kind that comes with a crib.

To make space, my desk had been squeezed up against my dresser, and my bed was so close to my closet that I couldn't get the door all the way open.

Sadly I walked in and sat down. I only looked around a second before burying my head in my pillow. My big, spacious room had turned cramped and teeny.

"Peekapoo!"

Thomas had crept into the room. He was lifting up the end of my pillow.

"Peekapoo! I see you!" he rhymed this time.

I groaned. "Boo," I corrected. "It's peekaboo."

Excitedly Thomas jumped on my back. "Look, Charrulls! Look at my stuff over there!"

He really liked me. I don't know why, but he did.

As quickly as he had jumped up, he jumped back down, ran over to his bed, and pointed. "See, Charrulls? I'm going to sleep here and you're going to sleep there. And it'll be just like when I spent the night at my friend Jeffrey Pete's house and then Mr. Pete had to come in four times and say 'Quiet down, boys,' and then we kept on laughing and then the next time he took Jeffrey Pete to the guest room."

This is how Thomas talks. His whole life is held together by "and thens."

As he was running around, Ben came in carrying three more cartons. When Thomas saw them, he went nuts.

"My toys! My toys! We packed them in those boxes, right, Dad? I was wonderin' where they were!"

As Ben left, my mother hurried through the doorway. She was wearing a bandanna over her hair. A bandanna means my mother's serious about cleaning. I think she wears it so she won't get mop water on her head.

She walked over to the closet and opened the door as far as it would go. Then she scanned the floor and let out a loud groan.

"I was afraid of this," she grumbled, turning to me. "This closet has *got* to be cleaned out, Charlie. Ben is going to build some more shelves. But for right now, we need to stack Thomas's toys and games on the floor in there."

I gave her a blank stare. Of all the chores in the entire universe, cleaning out my closet is the one I hate most. Besides, it didn't have to be done today, did it? Today was bad enough without adding the worst chore in the universe.

"*Now*, Charles. *Today*," she ordered, as if she had read my mind. "I want to get as much of this stuff put away as we can."

I continued to stare. What was wrong with her anyway? Couldn't she see what had happened to my big, spacious room? Wasn't that enough for her?

She folded her arms and squinted at me. "Charllllie," she said, as if lengthening my name would get me going. "The *closet*."

It made me mad. It really did.

"I can't," I said smugly. "There's a hand living in there."

It was the wrong thing to say. Mom glared at me a minute more, then stormed out of the room. A second later she was back with a box of giant plastic trash bags. She opened the first one so I could see how much it would hold. Then she disappeared into the closet and began filling it with the stuff on the floor.

I could hear it. Stuff I hadn't seen for years was being deposited in the bags for the garbage. That's where she would put it, too. My mother can be a very unreasonable person.

Just then I heard my xylophone crash to the bottom of the bag. It made me wince. I've always liked that xylophone. I realize it's a baby instrument, but I can still play "Three Blind Mice" and something else.

I got off the bed. "Okay, okay, okay!" I told her. "You win. You *always* win."

She stood up and looked at me. "You're the one who's making it into a battle." Then she handed me the bag and left.

After a few minutes of sifting through old papers and dirty socks, I found my xylophone. I couldn't find the little wooden mallet to play it with, but after searching the floor, I found a spoon. I think it was left over from a chocolate pudding I had a few months ago.

I started to play "Three Blind Mice." Just when I got to "See how they run," Thomas came back into the room. He dashed over to the closet door and started to sing.

I stopped playing right away.

Thomas finished the song without music. Then he pointed at my xylophone. "I don't have one of those," he informed me.

I knew what was coming next.

"Maybe I could have that one."

I shook my head no.

Without wasting a second, he scurried over to my desk and picked up my globe again. "How 'bout this? Can this be mine now? Can we share it?" He spun it around and around. "I really like this thing."

I put my head in my hands. I hate sharing. I know it's not the way you're supposed to feel, but I do. I don't think I'm alone, either. I think there are millions of kids all over the world who hate it as much as I do.

Sharing is not normal. If you don't believe me, just look at any *National Geographic* special. Name one lion who spends an entire day killing a zebra and then calls his friend over and says, "Here, Leo. I just spent ten hours chasing this zebra all over Africa. Help yourself."

Face it. The only time lions like to share is when they're already finished eating. And to me, that's not sharing. That's full.

Suddenly I stood up and hurried over to the three huge boxes in the middle of the floor. "Thomas," I said loudly to make sure I had his attention. Then I began touching each box with my finger.

"This box is yours. This box is yours. And this box is yours."

Before he could say anything, I rushed over to his bed and chest. "These are yours, too, Thomas. This is your bed and this is your little white chest. And all the stuff in the drawers is yours, too."

Thomas nodded happily.

"But that's all, okay, Thomas? Everything else in this room is mine."

I started to point. "The bed over there is mine, and that dresser is mine and all the stuff in the closet is mine, too. And the stuff on my desk and the posters on the wall. It's all my stuff, Thomas. And I'm not trading it, or sharing it, or mixing it together with your stuff. It's not even going to be both of ours. It's just going to stay mine."

Thomas was getting it now. "Oh," he muttered weakly. Then he gazed longingly over to my globe again. "I really liked that pretty blue world."

He wasn't angry. In all the time I'd known him, I'd never really seen Thomas angry. When things weren't going his way, he just seemed disappointed, and maybe kind of sad, I guess.

I softened a little.

"Okay, okay. I guess you can touch it once in a while," I conceded. "But only if you really feel you have to. And no spinning it out of control. Those are the globe rules."

Thomas smiled appreciatively and bobbed his head up and down. "I promise," he said gratefully.

He started to sit down on my bed. Then he realized his mistake and went to his own bed.

Lydia stuck her head in the door. She was carrying a small carton to her new room down the hall.

"Hi. What're you guys up to?"

Thomas frowned thoughtfully. "We're findin' out what's ours."

Lydia came in and plopped down on my bed. "Wow. You're totally squished in here, aren't you?" she observed. "Like a couple of sardines."

I know she didn't mean to be rubbing it

in—about having her own room and all—but I still wasn't in the mood to talk about it.

I left.

I hurried downstairs and passed through the living room. My mother was flitting from one corner to another trying to figure out where to put Ben's antique lamp. When she saw me, she raised her eyebrows.

"Closet cleaned?"

I nodded my head and kept on walking. I didn't stop till I was outside. I climbed up the fence and boosted myself onto the roof. Carefully I made my way toward the chimney. Once I got there, I sat down with my back against the bricks. I didn't want to spy. I just wanted to be alone.

I can't explain why, but being on the roof helps calm me down. I feel free up there or something. Like no one can get to me. And even if someone yells at me, it just floats away into space.

After about ten minutes Ben came strolling out back. My mother must have sent him to check on me. It was sort of interesting to watch how he did it. First he walked all the way to the fence and pretended to be looking at the garden. Then, trying to act casual, he slowly raised his eyes toward the roof. I stared down at him. I didn't smile or wave. I just sat and stared.

Quietly Ben walked back inside.

(five)

DON'T ASK me why, but every day Thomas seemed to like me more and more. My mother said I should have felt flattered that he followed me around so much, but I didn't. It would be like wading through a swamp and coming out with a leech on your leg. You would never really feel proud that you're the one it picked.

Everywhere I went, Thomas went. Once he even tried to follow me into the bathroom.

"No!" I told him sharply. "Not the bathroom. No."

I went in alone. When I came out, he was sitting by the door. He stood up and held his nose.

By the end of the second week I thought I would go crazy. One afternoon, just to have some privacy, I shut myself in the laundry room. I was only in there five minutes before Thomas slid open the door. He asked me to spin him around in the dryer.

Even my best friend Martin Oates and I couldn't play in private. Martin moved into the neighborhood last year from North Carolina. Since then, the two of us have stuck together like glue. My mother says it's getting hard to tell us apart. This is only funny if you know Martin is black.

Martin is about the coolest kid I've ever known. You should hear his accent. It's real slow and calm, like nobody in the world can rattle him. Also, he walks cooler than anything. Like he owns the street or something.

Thomas liked Martin almost as much as he liked me. Right from the beginning he'd follow him around the house like a shadow. Finally we gave up playing at my house and mostly just hung around the Oateses'. Martin has three sisters, but if they walk in his room, Martin throws a shoe at them, so they pretty much leave us alone.

Not Thomas, though. The few times we tried to play at my house, Thomas was a royal pain in the you-know-where. I'm serious. As soon as he'd find out Martin was coming over, he'd stand by the door to wait.

"He's coming! He's coming!" he'd scream as soon as he'd spot him. "It's that guy, Martin!"

Right after the Russos moved in, Martin came over to play Monopoly. Boy, was Thomas a pain *that* day!

"Hey! What're you guys gonna do? Can I do it with you guys? Can I? Can I, huh?" he started before Martin was even in the door.

I shook my head. "No. You can't do it with us, Thomas."

"We're playing Monopoly," Martin explained. "It's only for ages eight to adult. Look, it says so right here on the box."

"It's a law," I added just for good measure. "You could get arrested if you played."

Thomas laughed like he didn't believe me. "Hey! I know what. I can do the dice."

"Nope. Sorry. Can't," I stated clearly.

But even then, Thomas followed us into the room. He scrambled onto his bed and folded his hands on his lap. "I'll just do this, then."

I wanted to scream. Why wouldn't he get the message?

Martin turned his back so Thomas couldn't see. "Hit him with your shoe," he advised quietly.

I have to admit I felt like it. If we had been real

brothers, I probably would have tackled him and dragged him out of the room. But Thomas didn't feel like a real brother. He felt more like an uninvited guest. The kind of guest you're not supposed to clobber or your mother will kill you.

Finally Martin and I decided to try and ignore him. We figured if we didn't pay any attention to him, maybe he'd get bored and go away.

I don't mean Monopoly is boring, because it's not. Monopoly is my favorite game. For a while Martin and I played it almost every day. The best part is when the other guy is almost broke and he lands on your most expensive property and you get to jump up and scream, "Ha-ha! I'm rich! I'm rich!" The worst part is when you get into a giant brawl about trading properties and Martin throws the board out your bedroom window. So far that's only happened to us once.

After the money was handed out, Martin and I chose our playing pieces. As usual, I took the thimble and he took the shoe.

Still sitting on the bed, Thomas craned his neck to see into the box. The next thing I knew, he was on the floor sorting through the rest of the playing pieces. After touching each one, he finally grabbed the little toy iron and the top hat and scurried back to his bed.

I ignored him.

We rolled the dice to see who would go first.

"Two!" bellowed Thomas, who was really stretching his neck to the limit. "You got two, Charrulls!" He held up two fingers for our observation. "This many."

I ignored him.

Martin rolled.

"Hey! How many's that, Martin?" squealed Thomas. "That's a whole bunch, right? You got more than Charrulls. A lot more!"

I ignored him.

Martin started his shoe around the game board. Every time he touched down, Thomas counted out loud.

"One, two, three, four, five, six, seven, eight! Eight! Martin got eight!"

I ignored him.

Martin had landed on Vermont Avenue. "I'll buy it," he said.

"Buy it? Buy what? What're you going to buy, Martin? Where's your money? Are you going to use that play money, do you mean?"

This time I couldn't stop myself. I whipped around and stared at him. "I thought you were just going to sit there," I snapped.

Puzzled, Thomas looked down at himself. "I *am*, Charrulls. I *am* just sitting here. See?" Quickly he folded his hands again.

"I know, Thomas. But you're not being quiet. If you sit there you have to be quiet."

He frowned. "It doesn't say so on the box."

"Yes, it does," I said, picking up the lid. "It's right here: All children under age eight have to be quiet."

Martin grabbed the box lid and added, "If they talk, you must call the police."

Martin and I both started laughing over that one. Thomas laughed too, but I'm still not sure he knew it was a joke. Five-year-olds will believe practically anything.

For the next few minutes things got better. While Martin and I continued around the board buying real estate, Thomas just sat on his bed with his hands folded in his lap. Every once in a while I'd glance in his direction. It was a little bit pathetic, but not that much.

I was just beginning to enjoy myself when the humming started. It was quiet at first. Hardly even noticeable. But it was definitely humming and it was definitely coming from Thomas.

Ignore it, ignore it, I thought to myself. But after only a few seconds, Thomas increased the volume and added words.

"Ironing my pants . . . ironing my pants . . . ironing my pants."

I turned around. He was pretending to iron his

jeans with the little iron he had taken from the box. When he saw me looking, he put the little top hat on his head.

"How do you do, sir?" he said, making his voice real deep and tipping the hat in my direction.

Martin started to laugh. I wish he hadn't, but he did. Suddenly Thomas thought we were all having a good time. Before I knew it, he had scooted off his bed and was into the play money.

"Hey. I got an idea," he chirped happily as he plopped down. "Let's pretend that I'm the richest man in the world and that my name is Carl and that this is all my money and"—he paused to stuff some bills into his pocket—"and you guys are real poor and then you come to my house and you say, 'Carl, could we have some money?' and then I give you each two blue ones and a green one."

He stopped and handed Martin and me two fifties and a twenty.

That did it. Without even thinking, I jumped to my feet and ran downstairs. Since it was Saturday, my mother was cleaning the kitchen. She was standing next to the opened refrigerator holding something with mold on it.

"This isn't fair," I blurted. "It's not working. He's driving me crazy."

Mom made a face at the moldy thing and put it on the table. "Who?" she asked absentmindedly as she peered into the vegetable bin.

"Who? Who do you think? Thomas the Leech, that's who. Thomas the Bloodsucking Leech. Martin and I can't even play a game. He said he'd just sit there and shut up. But he won't. He counts and hums and sings and . . ."

Mom pulled out something squishy and ran it over to the sink. I still didn't have her attention.

I stormed to the phone. "I'm calling the police."

For the first time, my mother stopped what she was doing and looked at me. She was rolling her eyes, but at least she was looking.

"He likes you, Charles," she said, offering the same stupid excuse she'd used a hundred times before. "He just wants to be—"

I covered my ears. "No. I don't care about what he wants. That's all you ever say. About how much he likes me and how much he wants to be my brother. But I don't care about that, okay? I'm having him arrested."

Slowly she sank into the chair behind her and covered her face with her hands. My mother does this sort of thing a lot. Sometimes I think she's making faces at me under there.

Finally she breathed a big sigh and stood back

up. She put the moldy thing back inside the refrigerator.

"Okay," she said wearily. "I'll see what I can do. Send him down. Tell him I'll play a game of Candyland with him."

Relief spread across my face. The thrill of victory! I could hardly believe it! I'd won. At last she had listened to my side!

I was up the stairs in a flash. Breathlessly I delivered the good news.

"Thomas! My mom wants you. She wants you to bring your Candyland game downstairs and play with her."

He gave me a blank stare.

"Now! Right now!"

Without wasting another second I hurried to the closet, grabbed the game, and shoved it into his arms. "Go, Thomas! Hurry! She's waiting!"

Reluctantly Thomas got to his feet.

"Why?" he asked meekly.

I put my hand on his shoulder. "Never question adults," I said solemnly. And leading him by the hand, I ushered Thomas out of my room.

Martin and I began to laugh. We gave each other a high five, a low five, and a regular five.

The game started again. I landed on the B&O Railroad and Waterworks. I bought both of them. Martin got sent to jail. My luck was changing.

I had just landed on Boardwalk when I heard it. A creak on the stairs. Martin heard it too. We looked at each other. Then I closed my eyes as tight as they would go. No. Please, I prayed. Please don't let it be . . .

"Hi, guys."

I slumped to the floor.

Thomas was in the doorway. He was waving.

Standing behind him was my mother. A sheepish grin was pasted on her face. She motioned for me to come into the hall.

I folded my arms. This had better be good.

Casually she shrugged her shoulders. "He didn't want to play," she explained simply.

That was it? That was her excuse?

"What's that got to do with anything?" I growled. "You're the mother. Make him play."

Mom pulled me farther away from the door. Her expression grew more serious. "Listen, Charlie. You've got to understand this. It's not the same with Thomas as it is with you. I don't want to make him play if he doesn't want to. I don't want to be the bad guy. Not yet, anyway. Not over this."

She paused a second. "You and I have had years to build our love. We're sure of each other. Even when I'm a little hard on you, you still know I love you. But Thomas and I are just starting out. It takes time to build up that kind of love. And I just have to handle things a little differently with him right now."

She smiled weakly and tried to ruffle my hair. I backed away.

"Please try to understand," she said.

I didn't have to try to understand. It was simple. Thomas mattered more than I did. What was so hard about that?

I went back into my room. Thomas was stuffing more money in his pocket. He was already back to pretending.

"... And pretend that I'm famous, and then you bring your little children over to see me, and then you say, 'Carl, could we have some money to take our little children to Disneyland?'"

"I'm not calling you Carl," I snapped.

Then I stooped over and dumped the Monopoly game back into the box.

I motioned for Martin. "Come on. Let's get out of here."

Thomas's face dropped.

"Where? Where're you guys going?"

No one answered.

"Wait! Who am I gonna play with?"

Martin and I were almost out the door when it hit me. I turned around.

"I know who you can play with, Thomas.

There's a hand living in the bottom of the closet," I told him. "A hand and part of a wrist under my pile of clothes. Why don't you go in the closet and let it find you?"

Thomas's face lost its color. I'm not kidding. His eyes grew as big as saucers.

I didn't stick around to find out what happened next. I just grabbed Martin and got out of there.

I know it was mean, but I couldn't help it— that's how you act when you find out your feelings don't matter to your own mother.

Anyway, it's not like I got away with it. Thanks to Thomas, when I got home that afternoon I got the biggest lecture of my life. Thomas had been so upset about the hand, he made my mother call Ben home from work to search the closet. The two of them had to go through it inch by inch with a flashlight.

That night, Thomas made Ben put Mickey Mouse night lights in every electric plug in our room. Even then, he wouldn't go to bed until I did.

"There's no hand. There's no hand," he kept muttering to himself as the two of us entered the room. "It was just a little joke. Right, Charrulls? There's no hand in the closet."

Not at night, Thomas, I thought. At night it sleeps under your bed. I didn't say it, though.

Thomas made a giant leap for his bed and quickly ducked under the covers.

"You're mad at me, aren't you, Charrulls?" he whispered after a few seconds. "You're not talking to me."

I didn't answer. I just stood at the window looking out at the roof.

"Sorry," he said.

I'm not even sure he knew what he was apologizing for.

But I wasn't about to feel sorry for him. Why should I? It wasn't just my day he had ruined. It was my entire life.

"You're a tattletale, Thomas," I told him finally. "I don't want a tattletale for a brother."

I opened the window and crawled out. "And don't follow me out here. This is the only place I have left that's mine."

Quickly I crawled to my favorite spot by the chimney. The night air was chilly, but it felt good to be out of the house. I breathed in deeply and leaned back far enough to see the stars.

Time, I thought. Time was the magic word, right? At least according to most adults, time is all you ever need to make things better. "Give it some time," they'll say, "and everything will fall into place."

Only this time nothing was falling into place. It

had been almost a month and things were just getting worse.

I was getting worse, too. I knew I was. I was meaner and angrier than I'd been in a long time.

Suddenly a small gust of wind came from nowhere and made me shiver. I pulled my knees up close to my body and buried my head in my arms.

Huddling close to the chimney, I tried to remember the last time I had felt peaceful inside, and happy. I'm eleven, and I couldn't remember.

(six)

ON THE way to school the next morning I was still upset.

"I can't believe that little nerd told on me like that," I growled as Martin and I stood on the corner waiting to cross the street. "Can you? Can you believe he squealed? What a jerk!"

But instead of answering, Martin just folded his arms and looked at me. It was the kind of look an adult gives you when you're being a brat.

"Stop doing that," I said, annoyed. "I hate it when you do that. You look like my father."

Martin didn't change his expression. "I just feel sort of sorry for the kid, that's all. You probably scared the little dude out of his skin. I bet he didn't even mean to get you in trouble. He just didn't want some hand crawling out of the closet without its body."

"Oh, great. That's great, Martin," I snapped. "Thanks for all the support."

"Don't get mad about it. I'm not saying I want him hanging around us all the time or anything. All I'm saying is you can't really blame a little kid for being scared like that. After my sister Olivia saw *Frankenstein* for the first time, all you had to do was sneak up behind her and she'd wet her pants."

"Yeah, I know, Martin. You've told me that before. You still make fun of her about it, too. That's how understanding *you* are."

Martin just shrugged in that cool way of his. "Olivia's different. She isn't human. Olivia is a creature that my mother and father created to destroy me."

We stopped talking about it after that. That's the good thing about Martin. He tells me I'm wrong and then he quits. He doesn't keep lecturing the rest of the day like my mother usually does. In this case it didn't really matter, though. The junk Martin had said stayed in my head anyway.

I thought about how Thomas was only five and

how I had been treating him and how I was new to him, too. And about how I'd known all along I wasn't being very fair to him. After all, it wasn't his fault that my mother and Ben got married. Even if I'd really hated the kid, which I didn't, I had to admit that much. Maybe not to Martin, but to myself at least.

I DECIDED to try. I'm not kidding. For the next few days I was so patient and understanding with Thomas that I almost got an ulcer from the stress. Like at breakfast, when I saw him digging his dirty little paws into the bottom of the cereal box to get the toy surprise, I hardly even groaned. And later in the week, when he got frustrated over making his bed, I helped him smooth out the lumps. All I did was take his teddy out from under the covers, but he still hugged me for it.

The thing that really got me in trouble, though, was letting him sit in the chair with me while we watched *Wild Kingdom*. It made him think we were buddies.

"Thanks, Charrulls!" he exclaimed when he got down. "Thanks for letting me sit with you. That was fun, wasn't it?"

"Yeah, sure," I mumbled as I headed to my room.

"Hey! I got an idea!" he squealed, tagging along

behind. "Want to play something? Want to play Let's Pretend?"

Let's Pretend was Thomas's favorite game. It wasn't really a game, though. Thomas would just make up a bunch of dumb stuff to act out and you'd do it. I'd seen Lydia play it with him once or twice when she was baby-sitting.

"Please, Charrulls? Please?" he begged.

I filled my cheeks with air and let it seep out. "Okay, Thomas," I agreed reluctantly. "I'll play. But only for a little while."

It almost killed me to say it, but I did.

His eyes lit up like it was Christmas or something. "You mean it, Charrulls?"

"Don't push it, okay?" I said. "Let's just do this and get it over with."

He thought for a second. "I know! I've got a great one!" he exclaimed. "Let's pretend that I'm a magic guy and my name is Carl and then you come to my house and then I turn you into a horse."

I gritted my teeth and sat down on my bed. "Okay, fine. I'm a horse. Now what?"

"No, Charrulls! That's not how you play! You've got to do it! You've got to come to my house!"

Already I felt my eyes start to roll back in my head. "Where's your house?"

Thomas hid behind the trash can.

"You have to knock," he explained.

I knocked.

"Hello, boy," he said in a deep voice. "My name is Carl. What's yours?"

Before I could answer, he leaned into my ear. "Say your name is Wendell."

I frowned. "Could we just get on with this, please?"

Thomas nodded. "Okay, okay. Pretend I get mad at you for knocking on my door and then I decide to change you into a horse."

I looked at him strangely. "Heck of an idea, Carl."

Thomas frowned and shook his head. "No, Charrulls. You have to beg me not to do it. You have to say, 'Please, Carl. Please don't change me into a horse!'"

He looked at me and waited.

I took another deep breath and looked around to make sure no one was listening.

"Please, Carl. Please don't change me into a horse," I said finally.

Thomas made his voice real deep. "Yes, Wendell. I must."

Then he made a loud zapping noise.

"Okay, now pretend you're a horse and your name is Jellybean."

I covered my face with my hands. This was turning out to be even more humiliating than I had imagined. "I don't want that name," I told him.

"Yes," he said matter-of-factly. "Your name is Jellybean and you're a nice horse and you get down on your knees and ride me around the room."

He stood there patiently waiting again.

I know it's hard to believe, but I did it. I'm serious. I actually got down on my hands and knees and let Thomas get on my back. We circled the room two times.

"Whoa, Jellybean. Whoa, boy," he said at last, pulling back on my hair.

"Okay," he said as he got off. "Now pretend you get mad and you try to trample me and then I poke you with a stick."

I probably don't need to mention that this was something I *really* didn't want to do.

Once again, Thomas waited.

I was still thinking it over when he poked me under the arm with his finger.

"Come on. Do it."

A second later he poked me again. This time I knocked his hand away.

"Hey, Jellybean! Quit that!" he ordered.

It was degrading. It really was.

"I don't think I want to play this anymore, Thomas," I said. "Thanks a lot, though. It's been fun."

Thomas started to panic. "Yes, Charrulls! Yes! You have to!"

I just knelt there, looking at him. "Sorry, Carl. I just can't," I said quietly. Then I stood up and left the room.

Lydia was coming in the front door. Teenagers are always coming in from somewhere, but they never tell you where.

Upstairs, Thomas had started screaming, "Hey you! Come back here! Come back!"

As Lydia and I passed on the steps she stopped to listen. "What's wrong with him?" she wanted to know.

"Nothing," I muttered, continuing on my way.

She turned and followed me down to the living room. "Well, if nothing's wrong, then why is he yelling?"

I picked up the remote control and flipped on the TV. "We were playing a game and I quit, that's all," I said, trying to be real casual about it.

Lydia started to grin. "Was it Let's Pretend?" she asked.

Naturally I refused to admit it.

"Don't tell me. He was making you be a horse. Am I right?" she questioned.

Geez! Had she been spying the whole time or what?

"Jellybean?" she persisted.

"Great!" I said finally, throwing my hands in the air. "That's just great. You were listening."

Lydia laughed out loud. "How could I have been listening? I wasn't even here!"

"I don't know. But Martin Oates says that girls are the snoopiest, sneakiest busybodies in the world."

Lydia just kept grinning. "Get serious, Charles. I've been that stupid horse a million times myself. Every time I play with Thomas, he makes me be Jellybean."

Hearing this made me feel a little better. I pointed to my head. "Yeah, well, guess what? I think the kid's got a screw loose somewhere."

Suddenly Lydia's whole mood seemed to change. "He does not. He's just a little boy, that's all."

I shrugged. "Whatever."

I couldn't tell if she was really mad or what. Sometimes Lydia was a real puzzle. Half the time she acted like Thomas was a pest, and the other half, she was real protective of him, like a mother would be. Once she held a Kleenex while he blew his nose. You've got to practically worship somebody to do that.

For a while we just sat there quietly staring at the TV. But I knew that neither one of us was paying any attention to it. Lydia still had something else to say. I could feel it building up in the silence.

"Thomas hasn't had it that easy, you know," she blurted out all at once. "You shouldn't be so hard on him. His life has been hard enough."

I squirmed in my chair. It was embarrassing, being yelled at like that.

"He never even knew our mother," she went on. "Just think what that must be like for a minute."

She paused, and her voice softened. "She was really cute, my mom was. She didn't look like a grown-up woman, exactly. More like a kid. That's where Thomas and I got our freckles. Daddy says she had one of those faces that never get old."

She stopped again, as if she were remembering. "Thomas was only six weeks old when she, well, when she got sick. He looks at her pictures sometimes. He knows that it's Mom. We've told him enough. But still, you can tell by his eyes that he's looking at a stranger."

I glanced over at her face. Her eyes were filling up with tears.

She wiped them and stared out into space.

"It's really hard, you know?" she added almost

in a whisper. "When I fill out forms at school, I write 'deceased' where Mom is supposed to go."

Tears started to run down her cheeks. This time she stood up and hurried out of the room.

"Sorry," she said. "Sorry."

"No . . . it's okay," I called after her. "Really."

I wished I could have told her that I understood. I didn't, though. How could I? How could anyone understand something as sad as that?

(seven)

THE NEXT day things seemed to be back to normal. Lydia's alarm went off at six A.M. Then, just like every other school morning, I heard her come padding down the hall in her fuzzy bunny slippers. The ones with the ears. Then the bathroom door closed and the sound of the lock echoed in the hallway.

That was that. Lydia wouldn't come out again until her ride to school started honking the horn. Even if Thomas and I had to go really bad, she wouldn't unlock the stupid door. The first week she moved in I made a wet spot on my Superman,

Man of Steel pajamas. I'll never really forgive Lydia for that.

The trouble was, even when I did get into the bathroom, it wasn't the same as it used to be. Makeup and hair junk and perfume were crammed everywhere. Sometimes there was so much crap I couldn't even find my toothbrush. Once when I picked it up, it had already been used. I still get queasy when I think about it.

Besides the bathroom mess, rubber bands with little hair balls in them could be found all over the house. Like suddenly, she would be walking through the house and get this uncontrollable urge to rip out her ponytail, hair and all. It was disgusting and scary at the same time.

There was one more thing, too. Lydia smelled. I'm not kidding. She would walk by, and suddenly this giant perfume cloud would fill the air and make you cough. It hung in the air for about twenty minutes. To breathe, you had to put a hanky over your nose.

I'm not exaggerating. One night at dinner Ben took a whiff of her and pretended to clear out his sinuses. Lydia got tears in her eyes and left the table.

She ran upstairs to take a bubble bath. She took at least two baths or showers a day. That's twice as many as I took the entire time I was at camp.

"Great!" she shrieked from the top of the stairs. "Thomas used all my bubble bath again! There was almost half a bottle left last night and now it's gone!"

Ben glanced at Thomas and frowned.

Thomas shrugged and shoved in another forkful of mashed potatoes.

"Did not," he mumbled.

Lydia stormed back down to the kitchen and held the empty bottle upside down.

"Look at this! It's totally gone! He must have had bubbles up to the ceiling!"

Thomas kept right on eating.

"Did not," he repeated quietly. A kernel of corn fell out of his mouth onto the place mat.

"Yes, you did! You did too!"

This time Thomas looked up and smiled. "Not, not, not," he said.

"Too! too! too! too! too! too! too!" shrieked Lydia.

I excused myself from the table. Fights at dinner cause indigestion. And besides, I had enough problems of my own without getting involved in this one.

But just in case anyone wants my opinion, if Lydia had wanted to keep her precious bubble bath to herself, she shouldn't have put it right out on the tub in plain sight. It's not like it had her name on it or anything. Who knew?

And anyway, if the stupid bubbles had lasted longer, I wouldn't have needed so much.

UNFORTUNATELY, Lydia hogged more than just the bathroom. She was also a telephone hog. I'm not sure which was worse. When you think about it, the telephone and the toilet are a lot alike. You might not use them that often, but when you need them, you *need* them.

One night, because of Lydia's blabbing, I had to walk home from Martin's house in the pouring rain. I tried for an hour and a half to call my mother to come get me. That's ninety straight minutes! And all I could get was a busy signal!

Getting a busy signal for an hour and a half makes a person crazy. I'm not kidding. I read about a guy who got so mad at a busy signal that he shot his telephone right in the receiver. He said it was self-defense. I can understand that now.

Anyway, it finally got to be dinnertime and I was forced to leave. Mrs. Oates invited me to stay, but she was having vegetable casserole. I had it once. It made me spit up.

By the time I walked the two blocks to my house that night, I was soaked and shivering.

Also, my underwear was blue from my wet jeans.

Lydia was off the phone and back in the bathroom. Ben made her get out so I could take a hot bath. When she walked past, I gave her a dirty look.

"Thanks for staying on the phone all night," I growled.

Lydia looked at me and gasped.

"Oh wow! That reminds me. I haven't called Amanda back yet!"

I wore the underwear in the tub, but the blue never came out.

THE NEXT week I came down with the flu. I got it from the rain. My mother said you can't catch the flu from the rain but I did.

Ben and Lydia caught it first. I don't know where they got theirs, but they both got sick on Sunday. I didn't get sick until Wednesday. By then, all of my mother's sympathy had already been used up.

"You don't have a temperature," she informed me Wednesday morning when I said I didn't feel good.

"I don't care. I'm still sick," I told her.

She checked the thermometer again. "Why don't you go to school and give it a chance? See how you feel at lunchtime," she suggested.

I shook my head. "I can't. I'll be dead by lunchtime."

This time she frowned. "I want you to give it a try, Charlie. I've got to go into the office today and Ben's got his hands full with Lydia. Two sickies is just about all this family can handle."

"Oh, excuse me," I snapped. "Next time I'll wait my turn so I won't inconvenience anyone."

"Don't be so dramatic," Mom continued. "You know how you are. Sometimes after you get moving around a little bit, you start feeling better. If you don't, you can call me at work. You know the number of the real estate office, right? If you call, I'll come get you. I promise."

There was no sense arguing. Her mind was made up. I was going to school and that was that.

It turned out just like I knew it would. By eleven o'clock my head was down on my desk. By eleven fifteen, I was scouting the room for emergency places to puke.

Suddenly I shot my hand into the air. My stomach told me to.

"I need to go to the nurse's office!" I blurted out from the back of the room.

My teacher looked up from her desk.

"Now!" I added urgently.

Mrs. Berkie got the message. She sprang up

from her seat, dashed down my aisle, and slapped a hall pass into my hand.

"Run like the wind," she told me.

Out in the hall I could smell the food from the cafeteria. Beef and bean burritos. I put my hand over my mouth and started booking down the hall.

By the time I hit Nurse Cook's office I was almost out of breath. I didn't even wait for her to ask what was wrong. I just flopped down on her cot and rolled up into a little ball.

She stared at me a moment, but I can't really say she looked surprised. I have a feeling that on beef and bean burrito day, scenes like this are pretty common.

She covered me with a blanket and put her hand on my forehead. "Not feeling too good, huh?" she asked.

"Your name?"

I moaned and answered at the same time.

"Stay here. I need to go get your emergency card," she said. "Be back in a minute."

A minute? Oh no! I couldn't last a minute! Deep breaths, I ordered. Lots of deep breaths and the sick feeling will go away. In and out . . . in and out . . . in and . . . up. It came up on breath number three. I barely had time to grab the trash can.

The nurse came back before I was finished. She stopped in the doorway and made a face. Personally, I think that this was very unprofessional.

"Are you okay?" she asked at last.

Oh, yes. I'm fine, I thought. I love barfing into school trash cans. It's a hobby of mine.

But instead of saying anything, I just nodded.

Nurse Cook gave me a wet paper towel and pointed me toward the sink. Then she held her breath and carried the can out of the room.

A few minutes later she phoned my mother at work.

"Sorry, hon, but your mother isn't in the office right now," she reported. "They say she's out looking at property."

She tried my father next. He wasn't in his office either.

I sighed deeply. "Try my house," I suggested weakly.

She stared curiously at my emergency card again. "But if both your parents work, who would be at home?"

I took a deep breath. I had no choice. I was finally going to be forced to say the word.

"My stepfather," I replied, feeling sicker than ever.

Nurse Cook dialed the number. "Busy," she reported. "I'll try again in a few minutes."

She did, too. She tried calling my house for more than an hour. But every single time her message was the same. "Sorry, hon," she'd say. "Your phone is still—"

"I know. You don't have to tell me. Busy," I would mutter weakly.

By one o'clock my head was splitting and I had the chills. I tried to stay warm, but every kid who wandered into the office lifted up the blanket to see who I was.

At one thirty, Nurse Cook drove me home. I think she was afraid I was going to die on her cot. When you're a nurse, you have to worry about stuff like that. A death doesn't look that good on your record.

I was never so glad to see my house in my life. All I wanted was to go upstairs, crawl under my covers, and shiver in private. I dropped my books on the first step and started up to my room.

"That you, Charles?" called Ben, sounding raspy. "School out early?"

Slowly I turned around. Then, holding my head so it wouldn't explode, I walked gently into the living room.

Ben was stretched out on the couch watching TV. He was covered by a giant quilt. Lydia was curled in a big pink blanket next to the phone. The receiver was slightly off the hook.

I stood there and stared in disbelief. She had probably been talking to one of her sick friends and hadn't hung it up all the way. I couldn't believe it. All this time and no one had even noticed. Hadn't they heard the loud beeping the phone makes when it's off the hook? How could anyone sleep through a racket like that?

I should have started yelling. After what I'd been through, I should have yelled my brains out. But I just couldn't. If I yelled, my head would have split open.

I started out of the room. Ben looked sort of green. "Wait. So, how was your day?"

This time I couldn't resist. "Great. It was just great, Ben. I ralphed in the nurse's trash can."

Then I turned toward Lydia. "Oh yeah," I added. "Nurse Cook tried calling, but . . ."

I pointed at the phone.

Right away, they both saw the problem. Lydia got this sheepish look on her face. "Whoops. Sorry," she said, replacing the receiver. "I didn't hear it beep or anything. I must have been in the bathroom."

Ben frowned at his daughter. "Lydia," he said sternly. But that was it. I'm serious. That's all the punishment she got.

After that I went right to my room and got into bed. Then I burrowed my head in my pillow and tried not to die until my mother came home.

She walked through the front door at four o'clock. Ben must have told her what happened. At four thirty she brought hot tea and chicken noodle soup up to my room on a tray.

"I'm working on the Jell-O," she told me. Then she sat down on the edge of my bed—carefully, so she wouldn't spill the soup—and gently rubbed the side of my cheek with her hand.

She put her forehead next to mine and smiled sympathetically. That's one good thing about my mother. Even when I'm contagious, she's never afraid to get close to me.

"Sorry about what happened today," she said softly. "You okay?"

"No. You promised you'd be there and you weren't."

"I know, Charlie. I'm sorry. I was called out of the office unexpectedly and—"

"I knew this would happen. I told you I was sick but you wouldn't believe me. You didn't even care."

My mother looked as guilty as anything. "I cared," she said, rubbing my cheek again. "I know you had a bad day, honey, but—"

A bad day? Was that the understatement of the year or what?

I rolled my eyes. "Losing your favorite pencil is a bad day, Mother," I interrupted. "Puking in a trash can is just a little more serious."

My mother knows when she's licked. She didn't bother making any more excuses. Instead, she just sat there quietly while I ate my soup.

Ben and Lydia called her. She shouted, "Be there in a minute!" but she didn't go right away.

For a little while, it was just her and me.

(eight)

I SPENT the weekend at my dad's. I still wasn't feeling great, but anything was better than being home with Thomas. At least my father didn't keep coming into my room saying "Pretend that I'm a doctor and my name is Carl and I get to give you a shot."

My dad tried to understand what I was going through. Even when I was sick and grouchy he was pretty patient with me.

"I hate it there. I hate it," I complained again and again. "Living with the Russos is like living in a loony bin. Thomas is actually a man named Carl and Lydia has a phone growing out of her ear."

Dad surprised me. Ordinarily he would have put his hand on my shoulder and said something like, "Oh, come on, son, it's not that bad." Or, "Just give it a few weeks, it'll get better." But this time he really caught me off guard.

He took a deep breath and let it out slowly. "If I could have you here with me, I would. I hope you know that."

For a split second my whole world lit up. Just the thought of it was enough to change my mood.

"Dad! That's it! Of course! That's the answer to my problems! I'll come here and live with you! Just you and me. It'll be great! Why didn't we think of this before?"

Dad looked puzzled. "We did, Charlie. We talked about it with your mom before this all happened. You said you didn't want to leave your old neighborhood or change schools or stay with a baby-sitter when I'm out of town."

He paused a second, as if he was trying to recall something else. "Oh yeah, and you weren't too crazy about the idea of sleeping in the living room forever either. Don't you remember that? It wasn't even that long ago."

Suddenly my world crashed back in on top of me again.

"Yeah . . . I remember," I said, glumly staring at

his pull-out couch. "I just forgot for a second, but I remember now."

It was pretty obvious that I was disappointed. Dad reached over and gave me a quick hug.

"Never any easy answers, are there, son?" he asked sympathetically.

I shook my head no. Not anymore, I thought sadly. Not since last year when you left.

I DIDN'T go home until four o'clock on Sunday. I would have stayed at Dad's for dinner, but he was having shrimp egg rolls, beets, and stewed tomatoes. Men eat like that when they're alone.

When I walked into the living room that afternoon, Mom and Ben were sitting on the couch. Thomas and Lydia were stretched out on the floor in front of them. Seeing them like that sort of took me by surprise. They just looked so much like a normal family without me there.

I stood in the doorway with my suitcase. The extra son with the extra father.

"Oh, good, Charlie!" my mother exclaimed when she saw me. She hurried over and gave me a hug.

In her hand was a magazine. "There's a great article in here. I found it in the dentist's office yesterday and I've been waiting for you to get home so I could read it to everyone."

I didn't bother to argue. My mother takes her magazine articles very seriously.

She clicked off the TV and looked around. "Is everybody listening? It's called 'Bonding with Your Stepchildren.'"

Thomas bolted up. He'd been watching some wildlife show and was pretty annoyed that Mom had just clicked it off.

"Hey! What happened to the snakes?" he hollered.

My mother smiled.

"In a minute, Thomas. Right now this is more important. The doctor who wrote this is a psychiatrist with five stepchildren. He's had a lot of experience with families like ours—you know, stepfamilies—and he's made some suggestions that I thought might be good to try."

Ben shifted uneasily in his seat.

"I'd rather watch the snakes," whined Thomas.

"Shh," shushed my mother, and she began to read.

"'It's a good idea for each parent to spend time alone with his or her new stepchild. This should be quality time set aside for just the two of them. By joining in a favorite activity together, they can get to know each other away from the pressures of the family. They can learn to confide in each other. Learn to trust. And it's through this trust that the bonding process can begin. . . .' "

When she had finished, Mom looked up from the magazine and beamed proudly. I'm not kidding. It was like she wrote it herself or something.

"Well?" she asked. "What do you think?"

Ben was still fidgeting. Slowly he shook his head. "I don't know, Janet. I think we're doing fine the way we are. Isn't it better to learn to blend together as a family than to split everybody up?" he asked.

Thank you, Ben, I thought secretly. Thank you for wanting to spend quality time alone with me.

Meanwhile, my mother looked up at the ceiling and grimaced.

"Spending time alone with each child is not splitting everybody up, Ben. If Thomas and I spend some time alone and we get to know each other better, how can that possibly split things up?"

Mom looked at Lydia and me. "What do you two think? Lydia? Charlie?"

Lydia shrugged. She was right in the middle of pulling one of her rubber bands out of her head.

I just stared blankly into space. Maybe sleeping on the couch at Dad's wouldn't be so bad after all. At least my father didn't need to be forced to love me.

Suddenly Thomas got up off the floor and stormed over to where my mother was sitting. Then he leaned right into her face.

"I said I want to watch the snakes, dammit!"

Hearing him swear took all of us by surprise. A big hush settled over the room and my mother's mouth dropped open. So did mine.

I tried to keep from laughing, but it wasn't easy. Especially when Ben grabbed Thomas by the arm and marched him up the stairs. Thomas knew he was in big trouble. The whole way to his room he kept saying, "I don't *have* to watch the snakes, Dad. Let's be friends. Do you want to be friends, Dad?"

When Ben finally came back downstairs, he walked over to my mother and put his arms around her. He did it right in front of Lydia and me.

"Looks like maybe we'd better give this guy's idea a try," he said, picking up the magazine.

Mom rested her head on his shoulder and whispered, "Thanks."

I left the room. It bothered me to see the two of them hug. I wouldn't have minded if Ben had given her a hearty slap on the back once in a while, but soft whispering and hugging—well, it just got to me, that's all.

THEY SET it up for Saturday. Ben and I would go fishing and Mom would take Lydia shopping and out to lunch. Thomas would go to his friend Jeffrey Pete's house. His turn would come next.

The more I thought about it, the less I wanted to go. What kind of personal junk was I supposed to learn about Ben, anyway? That he liked to stomp around in nature in a flannel shirt and eat Hungry Jack pancakes? That he went outside every night after dinner and watched the sun set? Okay, fine. So what?

And what about me? Was I actually supposed to confess my true feelings about his family? Should I tell him that I thought his son was a mental case, or that sometimes Lydia was unbelievably selfish? Would that "bond" Ben and me together?

Or how about this one? Would it help if I told Ben that sometimes when no one was around I went up to the attic and pulled out the box of pictures my mother had put away? The ones of her and Dad and me. And that I stared at them and tried to remember.

And that sometimes my eyes clouded up. Not

often, but it still happened. Should I tell him that, too?

BEN HONKED his horn. Reluctantly I walked downstairs and closed the front door behind me.

I got into the truck. Ben leaned over and gave me a pat on the knee.

I forced a smile, but it wasn't easy. The thing is, I don't even like fishing. It was Ben's idea. I know this doesn't make me seem like much of an outdoorsman, but it's true. The first time I ever went fishing I hooked my father in the neck and he took my pole away. The second time I caught a pair of boxer shorts and a plastic bag.

Ben pulled out of the driveway and turned on the radio. "Thought we'd go to Lake Murky," he said. "Ever been there?"

I nodded. Lake Murky. That's where I had caught my boxer shorts.

It wasn't a very long drive, but the two of us didn't talk much. Ben and I never do. My mother says he's not much of a talker, but I couldn't help wondering if he just didn't like me. Once the two of us were stuck in the car while Mom ran into the grocery store. Ben cleared his throat twice. It was one of our best conversations.

When we finally got to the lake, we unloaded the fishing gear from the back of the truck. Then we walked down to the boathouse. Ben bought some sandwiches and other stuff from the cooler and then rented a small motorboat.

You could tell he'd done a lot of fishing up there. Once we were in the boat, he knew right where to go. He drove to this little cove about ten minutes from the dock and turned off the engine.

"Best fishing spot on the lake," he informed me as he handed me a pole. Then he reached into the bait box and pulled out a fat wiggly red earthworm. It was the slimy kind that are squished all over the sidewalk after a hard rain.

"Here you go," he said.

I felt myself start to sweat. There aren't a lot of guys who will admit this, but worms sort of turn my stomach. I think it has something to do with them not having arms, legs, or a neck.

For a second or two I didn't know what to do. I tried to hold out my hand, but it just stayed tucked under my arm in a tight little fist. Meanwhile, Ben kept stretching his arm farther and farther for me to take it.

Finally I shook my head. "Er, no thanks. I, uh, don't use worms. I usually just use . . . well, uh, I just use . . ."

Geez, why couldn't I say it?

Curiously, Ben raised his eyebrows. He was waiting.

I ducked my head down and mumbled "Bologna" as quietly as I could into my sleeve.

Ben stared at me a second. "Bologna?" he repeated loudly. I'm not kidding. The word *bologna* echoed all over the lake.

I could feel my face turning red. What was the big deal, anyway? Last year Martin Oates caught a sea bass with a Vienna sausage.

Ben looked at me funny but he didn't laugh. "Sorry. No bologna. Try this."

He tossed me a fudge brownie that he'd bought at the boathouse. I tore off a small piece and rolled it into a ball. Then I put it on the end of my hook. I felt like I was fishing for Betty Crocker.

For the next two hours the two of us just sat there with our poles in the water. Some fun. Most of the time I think Ben was practically asleep. Once in a while, when my bobber would move, he'd open his eyes and say, "Got a nibble?" But it didn't actually make me feel bonded to him or anything.

Ben was the first to get a bite. As soon as he felt the tug on the line he sat up and began reeling it in—steady and calm like you're supposed to.

But even though he wasn't jumping up and down, you could tell he was getting a kick out of it. The whole time he was pulling it in, he kept whispering "Come to Papa, come to Papa."

"Get the net, Charlie," he ordered. "Quick! Scoop him in."

I leaned over and caught the fish in the net. It was flopping around like crazy.

I cringed when I saw the hook. "Gross," I said. "Right through the lip."

Ben took the fish and tried to twist the hook out of its mouth. Suddenly I felt queasy.

He looked up and saw my expression. "Don't worry. It doesn't hurt him."

"How do you know?" I asked.

Ben just kept twisting.

I covered my eyes with my hands. "It's kind of hard not to feel a hook through your mouth, don't you think?"

Ben didn't answer.

"I even feel it when I've got a crumb on my lip."

After a minute I peeked through my fingers. "Sure looks like it hurts, doesn't it? The way it keeps flopping around like that."

I leaned closer. "Oh geez, it's bleeding."

Seeing the blood made things even worse.

"What's the difference between fishing and murder, do you think?" I wondered out loud. "Do you think just because you eat it, it's not murder?"

Ben stopped what he was doing and stared at me. He didn't say anything. He just stared.

Finally the hook came out. "My guess would be that you won't be wanting to take this home and eat it, is that correct?" he asked, sounding a little exasperated.

I made a face at the thought of it. "You mean with that lip of his and everything?"

Ben threw it back. Then for the next few minutes he just sat there looking out over the water.

I guess I shouldn't have made him throw it back. I guess we should have taken it home and eaten it. I probably wouldn't have had to eat the lips.

Hoping to make things better, I cast my brownie back into the lake. Five minutes later I caught a Huggies diaper.

Ben started the outboard motor. We left.

On the way home the silence was louder than ever.

(nine)

THE LAST straw. That's what they call it when you run out of patience. I never used to understand why they called it that, but I do now. It's like if you're a camel and you have to carry a bunch of straw to market. And everyone thinks you're real strong, so they just keep piling more and more straws on your back. And even though your load keeps getting heavier and heavier and your legs start buckling underneath you, you just put up with it, because that's what they expect you to do.

Only finally you reach your limit. You don't know it's going to happen. But one day someone reaches up and puts one more straw on your back, and you collapse right on top of him. And he deserves it too. 'Cause he wasn't paying attention to how you felt. And everyone has a limit. Me and camels and everyone.

THOMAS started calling my mother Mom. He started doing it after their day "alone" together. I don't know if they talked about it or if he just did it on his own. All I know is that he was heading up to bed that night when he suddenly stopped on the stairs and said, "See you in the morning, Mom."

I'm not kidding. He said it real casual like that. As if calling a person Mom was hardly a big deal at all.

It really got to me. *Don't call her that!* I wanted to shout. She's *my* mother, not yours!

I THOUGHT about it that night. Not just about Thomas calling my mother Mom. I thought about all of it. About Lydia and Ben, and how much I'd given up, and how much I'd had to accept: sharing my room with a little kid, learning to live with a sister, giving both of them my mother, watching her love a man who wasn't my dad—a man who didn't even seem to like me that much. . . .

It felt heavy, you know? Like a ton of straw,

only worse. And even though I was in bed, I thought I felt my legs start to buckle under me. I'm serious. I could really feel them caving in.

I didn't sleep very well. I tossed and turned and woke up a million times.

Glum. That was my mood when I went down to breakfast the next morning. Not a good time to discover that Lydia and Thomas had eaten the last bowl of Fruity Flakes. When I looked in the cupboard all that was left was Ben's cereal. Fiber something.

I hurried into the living room and there they were. Thomas was curled up in the chair watching *Sesame Street*. Lydia was stretched out on the couch waiting for the phone to ring. They both looked full.

"Look, Charrulls," said Thomas excitedly as he pointed to the screen. "There's Bernie!"

I rolled my eyes. "How many times do I have to tell you, Thomas?" I said. "It's not Bernie. It's Bert and Ernie. They're two separate people."

"Puppets," corrected Lydia, raising a finger in the air.

I frowned. "Oh. Like I didn't already know that."

Just then my stomach started to growl. Not loud enough for anyone to hear, but enough to make me double over.

Lydia glanced at me curiously.

"My stomach's growling," I informed her curtly. "The reason it's growling is that no one left me anything to eat for breakfast. All the cereal's gone."

Casually she shook her head. "That's not true. There's other cereal in there."

I made a face. "Oh, boy. Bark and twigs."

Lydia shrugged again and turned back to the TV.

"The Fruity Flakes were mine," I persisted. "My mother bought them for me."

This time she looked at the ceiling and sighed in annoyance. "They were for *all* of us, Charles."

"No, they weren't," I argued. I could feel the anger building inside me. "They were just mine. I get to have something around here too, you know. You two don't get everything!"

Lydia's eyes grew wide. "Everything?" she snapped, bolting up. "What do you mean we '*get everything*'? What have we cheated you out of, Charlie? We gave up our whole house and our whole neighborhood to come here. What did you give up? Nothing, that's what! So excuse me if I accidentally had the last bowl of cereal, Your Majesty!"

I was trying to think of something smart to yell back at her when Thomas stamped his foot.

"Shh! Quiet!" he shouted. "I can't hear the Bernie with the long head!"

I covered my face with my hands. Like I said, the place was a loony bin.

"Bert," I muttered for the millionth time. "His name is Bert. Bert, Bert, Bert, Bert, Bert, Bert, Bert, Bert . . ."

Beep-beep! Outside, a loud car horn interrupted my Berts. I don't mean just one or two little toots, either. I mean major honking. Like little kids do when their mom leaves them in the car while she runs into the grocery store.

Thomas stood up in the chair and peeked through the window. "*Meemee!*" he shrieked. "*Meemee Russo!*"

The next thing I knew, he and Lydia were flying out of the living room headed toward the front door. That was that. I never even had a chance to finish my argument with Lydia. I could have thought of some good stuff, too. I know I could have.

Feeling more frustrated than ever, I stood up and looked outside. The honking was coming from a giant white car parked in our driveway. I'm not sure of the make, but it was the kind of car they call a gas guzzler. I'd seen it before at the wedding.

It belonged to Ben's mother.

In the time it took me to get to the window,

Mom and Ben had dashed from the back yard to greet her. Standing there with Thomas and Lydia, Ben opened her door.

Mrs. Russo got out of the car. Her cotton-candy white hair came first, about two feet of it piled on top of her head. It was the kind of hair that you could shoot a cannonball through and never get close to her scalp.

She hugged and kissed each one of them. Thomas's hug was the longest. He dangled from her neck until Ben poked him to let go.

In no time at all the five of them were headed toward the front door. I barely had time to make it to my room.

"Didja bring me something, Meemee?" Thomas squealed loudly as they came inside. "What d'ja bring me?"

"Here, Meemee. Sit here!" urged Lydia.

I rolled my eyes again. Meemee. Great name. I guess that made her my stepmeemee.

"Charles!" called my mother from the bottom of the stairs. "Charles, come down here! We have company!"

Darn! I knew she'd be calling for me! At our house, my mother treats every person who walks through the front door like royalty or something. Once she made a meat loaf sandwich for a guy selling spot remover.

I started to get dressed. Once I was safely in my clothes, maybe I could sneak onto the roof, lower myself onto the fence, and take off for Martin's house.

"Charles!" demanded my mother again. This time she was at the bottom of the stairs. "Come on down here! See who it is!"

I sighed and slowly sat down on the edge of my bed. There was no use trying to escape. Mom was being too persistent. Soon she'd be coming up to get me.

I still don't know what the big deal was. It wasn't like I was a part of the Russo family or anything. Not a *real* part, related by blood and everything.

I'll never forget when I walked into the living room that morning. Thomas jumped off the couch and started pointing at Mrs. Russo like this was the best thing that had ever happened to him.

"Look! Look! Surprise!" he squeaked. "It's my meemee! It's my meemee!"

You could tell Ben's mother really loved the attention. She was beaming from ear to ear.

"Why, there he is," she exclaimed pleasantly as she held out her hand to me. "How are you, Chuck?"

Chuck. I'm not kidding. She called me Chuck.

Thomas started to laugh. "Chuck? That's not Chuck, you silly. That's Charrulls! He lives with us now."

I turned toward Thomas and frowned. "You live with *me*, you mean," I corrected.

Mrs. Russo wasn't paying attention. Instead, she eyed me suspiciously. Then she turned to Ben.

"Don't they call him Chuck?" she inquired, as if I wasn't even in the room. "I could have sworn at the wedding they called him—"

"No. They don't call me Chuck," I interrupted. "I'm positive."

Ben caught my eye and winked. He was trying to make me feel better, but in my mood it didn't help.

After that, I sat down and listened while the rest of them talked over old times. As it turned out, Ben's mother was famous for popping in on them like that.

" 'Member last year when you surprised Lydia and me and took us to the beach for the weekend, Meemee?" Thomas reminded her happily. "That was fun, wasn't it? 'Member how you let me eat a banana split for dinner and then I got a hot fudge sundae for dessert?"

Suddenly he made a face. " 'Member how my stomach got upset and I spit up the cherry?"

(108)

"Oh, sick, Thomas!" exclaimed Lydia. "Gross. Why'd you have to remind us?"

Thomas started laughing. " 'Member that, Charrulls? That was funny, wasn't it?"

Before I could answer, he shook his head and corrected himself. "Whoops. Forgot. We didn't even know you then."

Mrs. Russo hit herself in the head and grinned. "I guess poor old Meemee doesn't even know him now."

Everyone laughed but me. Even my mother. Like not knowing my name had been the joke of the century.

"Are you gonna stay overnight, Meemee?" Thomas begged, folding his hands together like he was praying. "Please, please, please."

"Of *course* she's going to stay," insisted my mother. "We wouldn't have it any other way."

Mrs. Russo hesitated. "Oh, I don't know. I hadn't really planned on—"

"There's plenty of room for you, Mother," interrupted Ben. "Plenty of room."

I felt myself starting to frown. What room was he talking about? If there was so darned much room, why was I sharing mine?

"I know! I know!" squealed Thomas. "You can stay in my room with me! Right, Dad? Right, Mom?"

I bristled. He called her that name again.

"Hey! I got an idea! Meemee can sleep in Charrulls's bed! It'd be just like at the beach when I slept on that little cot in your room, Meemee!"

Suddenly all eyes turned toward me. I'm not kidding. It's like I was the North Pole and all the eyeballs in the room were magnets. My mother's eyebrows were raised like she was honestly wondering if this would be all right with me.

"I'm sure Charlie won't mind sleeping on the couch for a couple of nights," she said matter-of-factly. "That'd be okay with you, wouldn't it, honey?"

That was it. That was the last straw. Something inside me snapped. And when it did, words came spilling out of my mouth. Words I hadn't even had time to think about.

"Yeah, sure, that'd be perfect! Mrs. Russo can have my bed. Geez, what do I need a bed for? I hardly even have a room anymore."

I stood up and started to leave. "Hey! I've got an idea. I'll sleep under a rock in the back yard. Then I won't be in anyone's way at all. It'll almost be like I don't even exist."

As I started to turn the corner I suddenly stopped and looked back. This time I stared straight at my mom.

"By the way, Mother, I've got some memories,

too, you know. Like remember when we were a *real* family—you and Dad and me?"

My eyes darted to Mrs. Russo, then back again. "We used to go to the beach, too. We went there a lot. And Dad and I would ride the waves and have these contests to see who could go the farthest. He always let me win. I didn't know it then, but I do now.

"And sometimes Grandma and Granddad would drive down to the beach and see us for the weekend. And we'd have picnics in the sand and Grandma and I would look for shells.

"And they'd come for Thanksgiving, too. We were just like the families you'd see on those Butterball commercials. Granddad would carve the turkey and say this grace he made up about how lucky we all were to have each other. Remember that, Mom?"

My voice quieted to a whisper.

"Lucky me."

(ten)

I COULDN'T get out of there fast enough. I slammed the front door. I don't usually explode like that in front of strangers. Normally I save the worst behavior for those I love.

I headed for the park. Or maybe I should say the tree. The same tree where Mom and I had our last picnic and she told me nothing would ever come between us.

When I got about a block away, I started to run. I don't know why I felt in such a hurry to get there. I needed to think things over. But let's face it, all the thinking in the world wasn't going to change anything. It wouldn't solve my problems with Thomas or Lydia. It wouldn't even make Ben and me best friends. Thinking doesn't work miracles. Not even when you end with amen.

As I hurried down the park's sidewalk I couldn't help but notice how many people there were around. It kind of took me by surprise, since I don't usually go to the park on Sundays. But when I finally rounded the corner of the boys' bathroom and spotted the tree, I stopped dead in my tracks. I could hardly believe what I saw. It was covered with kids! Strange little kids were hanging all over its branches!

Hey! I wanted to scream. Get down from there! Out of the tree, you jerks! It's mine!

I didn't, though. It wouldn't have done any good. Two of the little kids had spiked hair and were wearing black rock-concert T-shirts. Kids like that don't listen to you unless you have a weapon.

Instead of yelling, I just stood there and watched my tree being overrun. Then I said a cuss word and left.

I started to walk. There was nowhere to go. I called my dad from Circle K. He wasn't home.

After I hung up, I tried Martin's. He was at a soccer game. I didn't call anyone else. I have other friends, but not the kind I needed.

I walked as slowly as I could—scuffing my feet—on my way to nowhere in particular. Like the homeless men you see walking on the street sometimes. I know I was overdoing it on the self-pity, but I couldn't help it. It's a wonder I didn't start collecting aluminum cans.

Walking is boring. Putting one foot in front of the other—that's all it is. My grandfather says that walking puts you in touch with nature. But to me, touching nature isn't that big of a thrill.

Finally my feet started aching and my stomach began to growl. There was no place to go except home. I guess I could have headed downtown to the homeless shelter, but I didn't have the guts. Besides, I have a feeling the homeless shelter is serious business. I don't think they give you a free meal just because your stepmeemee called you Chuck.

When I turned down my block, the first thing I noticed was that the gas guzzler was gone. So far it was the only high point of my day. I didn't know where she went, but I hoped she wouldn't come back.

I also noticed that Ben's truck wasn't there. I couldn't believe it. It was almost too good to be true.

I snuck up to the house and opened the front

door as quietly as I could. Once I was inside I stopped in the hallway to listen for voices.

Please, God, please, I prayed. Just let me get upstairs with no one seeing me. Amen.

The house was silent.

I looked up and whispered, "Thank you." I always look up when I pray. It's a habit from when I was a little kid. MaryAnn Brady told me that God lived on the ceiling.

Making a dash for the dining room, I grabbed two bananas from the bowl on the table. Then I ran to my room and closed the door behind me. Without wasting one more second I opened my window and climbed out onto the roof.

I stood there a minute and breathed in the cool air. I could already feel myself start to calm down.

I climbed higher and settled in my usual spot next to the chimney. I ate the bananas. Then I leaned back and felt the warm sun on my face. I closed my eyes and listened to myself breathing. That's how quiet it was up there.

My nose was making a little whistling noise. In and out . . . in and out . . . in and out . . .

Listening to your own breathing can almost put you to sleep. I guess it's just the rhythm of it or something. In and out . . . in and out . . . slow and steady . . . in and out . . .

Suddenly I felt myself tense up all over again. I covered my ears, but there was no sense pretending I hadn't heard it. Out front, Ben's truck had just pulled into the driveway.

Car doors opened and closed. Thomas's screechy little voice filled the air as he ran for the front door.

"Hey, Mom. I'm gonna see if Charrulls is . . ."

Even though the rest of the sentence was finished in the house, I knew what it was.

". . . home yet," I whispered, feeling sick.

Closing my eyes, I could picture Thomas frantically dashing around trying to find me. In my mind I could almost see where he was in the house.

The living room . . . the kitchen . . . flying down the hall to the stairs . . . taking them two by two . . . now rushing into the bedroom . . . looking around . . . giving the globe a spin . . . looking around some more. Aha! The opened window!

Slowly I began counting to five. I was only on four when Thomas leaned his big head out the window.

"Charrulls!" he exclaimed like he had just

made an important discovery. "There you are!"

He waved. I didn't wave back.

His leg came next. Then his other leg.

"Hey, Charrulls! Look at me!"

The loudness of his own voice seemed to throw him slightly off balance.

"Whoops," he said, holding out his arms to steady himself. He was really shaky. Like he was on a tightrope instead of an entire roof.

"Whoa, it's scary up here, huh, Charrulls?"

"Go back inside, Thomas," I told him. "Please. I just want to sit out here by myself for a while."

He acted like he didn't even hear me. Shaky and stiff-legged, he started inching his way toward me.

"Thomas. Go back inside," I repeated. "I mean it."

He hunched over to help balance himself against the steepness of the roof and kept coming. He couldn't seem to talk and walk at the same time.

"God, Thomas!" I finally yelled this time. "Why can't you just leave me alone? Why can't you ever just leave me alone?"

Finally, just inches from my foot, he stopped and looked up. His face was frozen in a tense, unnatural grin. There were drops of sweat on his top lip.

Slowly, almost in slow motion, he straightened up. "You shouldn't say God, Charrulls," he said quietly.

Then, still trembling, he studied the distance between us and inched one more step closer. I was just about to yell at him again when suddenly—with no warning at all—he lunged forward and grabbed for my foot.

"No!" I said as his hands reached for my ankle. I pulled my foot away. It was automatic. I didn't even think about it. I just saw him start to grab me and I pulled away.

Thomas fell.

It happened so fast I don't even remember much about it. Or maybe I just don't want to. That happens sometimes. You forget what you don't want to remember.

All I know is that the roof was steep and Thomas couldn't catch himself. And he slipped and rolled toward the edge. And then he was gone. Just like that. He fell.

I heard him hit the ground. I don't want to talk about it, but I heard that noise.

Sometimes when emergencies happen you freeze. You want to help, but you can't. Your brain won't tell you what to do. I saw a dog get hit by a car once. I couldn't even scream.

But this time was different. As soon as I saw

what was happening I slid to the window as fast as I could and pulled myself inside.

"Mom! Ben! Quick! It's Thomas!" I shrieked as loudly as I could. But outside Thomas had already started screaming. And my mother and Ben were racing out the back door to see what had happened.

I should have gone too. I know I should have. But for some reason I just couldn't bring myself to go down there.

Instead, I began frantically pacing back and forth on my floor. "At least he's yelling," I told myself. "At least he's not . . . well, quiet. Quiet is bad. Loud is good. Yelling is loud. Yelling is good. . . ."

I just kept babbling on and on like that. I couldn't stop. If I stopped, I might start to think. And if I started to think . . . well, I just didn't want to, that's all.

Suddenly downstairs there was a lot of commotion. Lydia came through the front door just as Mom and Ben were helping Thomas out to the car. Their voices mixed together in loud and confused conversation.

"Hey, what happened? Why's Thomas crying?"

"Here, son, here's a tissue. Hold his arm, Janet."

"Quick, Lydia. Open the front door."

"Somebody tell me what happened!"

"He fell. We're taking him to the emergency room. Are you doing okay, son? Here, wipe your nose. You okay?"

They whisked him out the front door. A second later Ben's truck pulled away. I ran to the end of the hall in time to see it turn the corner.

"Oh God, oh God, oh God . . ."

It's all I could say. It wasn't praying, exactly. But it wasn't cussing either.

"Oh God, oh God, oh God . . ."

I tiptoed back to my room. I got in bed and covered up with my bedspread. A second later I got out again. I paced a few more steps, sat down, sat back up, lay down, stood up, and finally buried my head in the pillow.

He's okay. Yeah, sure he is. No one yells that loud if they're not okay. It was just a little tumble, that's all. A little tumble off the roof. He landed on the grass, right? Grass is soft, right?

Tears filled my eyes. I hadn't meant to hurt him. Why would I want to hurt him? Just because I was upset? That didn't mean anything. Just because I was upset didn't mean I'd hurt him.

It was an accident. Yeah, of course it was. I'm positive. I never would have made him fall on purpose. I don't care if no one believes me, either. I wouldn't have done a thing like that. If I'd known Thomas was going to fall, I never would have pulled away from him the way I did. Honest to God. I wouldn't have.

I wiped my eyes and took a deep breath.

"Just let him be okay. Come on, God. He's only five. Just make him all right."

(eleven)

TWO HOURS. That's how long they were gone. Two hours that seemed more like ten.

As soon as I heard them pull into the driveway I raced downstairs. Lydia was just about to open the door. She looked surprised to see me.

"Where'd you come from?"

I strained to see outside. Thomas was walking up the porch steps with my mother and Ben. His arm was in a sling. Other than that, he seemed to be okay.

I raised my eyes toward the ceiling and said, "Thank you."

Lydia looked at me funny and said, "You're welcome."

After the three of them came inside, things got more confused than ever.

"What did you break, Thomas?" Lydia wanted to know. "What's wrong with your arm?"

Before he could answer, my mother looked at me and frowned. "Where have you been?" she demanded. "We were worried sick about you."

Anxiously Lydia pulled at the rubber band in her hair. "Will someone please tell me what he broke?"

"We didn't know where you were or who you were with or when you were coming home. You know better than to go storming off like that. You know how worried I get."

Lydia was about to explode.

"Collarbone," said Ben, finally answering her.

"Collarbone," echoed Thomas. "It doesn't hurt anymore. I woulda hada cast only they don't put a cast on collarbones. Right, Dad? I just get to have a swing."

"Sling," corrected Ben.

"Next time you pull a stunt like that you're going to be punished," continued my mother, waving her finger in my face.

Lydia still seemed frustrated. "How, though? How did he break it? You can't break your collarbone by just falling over in the grass."

Just for a split second Thomas looked at me. Then he quickly looked away.

"Can too," he said quietly.

Lydia's expression grew angry.

"No, you can't, Thomas!"

"Can too, can too," he repeated just as calmly.

Lydia threw her hands in the air and left the room in a huff.

Ben shook his head. "Didn't take long to get back to normal, did it?"

My mother was still glaring at me. "You and I aren't done yet, bucko," she said. I'm serious. She actually called me bucko.

Ben took her arm and pulled her toward the kitchen. "We'll finish this discussion at dinner," she called, still waving her finger.

I just sighed.

Thomas sat down on the couch. He didn't turn on the television. He just started staring at his sling.

It made me feel sick inside.

I sat down next to him.

"I'm sorry, Thomas," I said softly. "I'm *really* sorry. I never meant for this to happen. It was an accident."

Thomas raised his head. He wasn't smiling exactly, but he didn't look mad, either.

He motioned for me to come closer. Like he had a secret or something.

Careful not to touch his sling, I leaned over next to him.

"I didn't tell, Charrulls," he whispered in my ear.

Puzzled, I raised my eyebrows.

"About what happened on the roof," he explained. "I didn't tattle like I did before."

Even then I didn't fully understand.

Thomas took an exasperated breath. " 'Member how you got mad at me when I told them that you said there was a hand in the closet? Well, this time I didn't tell them what happened. I didn't tattle about anything."

Suddenly I felt even worse than before. How could he have remembered that? How could it have been so important to him?

I didn't know what to say. I just sat there watching Thomas's face grow even more serious. Then, after what seemed to be the longest he had ever been quiet, he finally looked up at me and whispered, "Now you like me. Right, Charrulls?"

GUILT. That's one word I don't have to bother looking up in the dictionary. Everyone knows what guilt means. Guilt is the way you punish yourself when there's no one else to do it for you.

Guilt is a little voice inside your head that screams, "You should be ashamed of yourself!" And even though it's a silent voice, your whole body hears it. And it makes your shoulders slump over a little bit. And sometimes your chin drops down to your chest. And your feet drag when they walk.

That's what guilt does to me, anyway. I'm not kidding. When I finally left Thomas that afternoon, my head and shoulders felt so heavy I wasn't sure I could even get them upstairs.

Now you like me. Right, Charrulls?

I couldn't get it out of my mind. All the way up the steps it kept echoing around in my brain.

You ought to be ashamed of yourself! screamed the silent voice in between echoes. *Poor Thomas. Poor little Thomas.*

When I got to my room I didn't go inside. My feet kept right on going, straight down the hall to the attic door. I can't explain why. They just took me there.

I put my hands over my ears to try to shut out the voice. It wasn't any use, though. When the voice is inside, covering your ears just traps it.

I pulled on the light at the bottom of the staircase and carefully began edging my way around the stack of boxes piled high on the steps. It was dark at the top. There's another light I could have pulled on, but I didn't. Just the mood I was in, I guess. Besides, I know my way around the attic by heart. I know exactly where the pictures are. Even if it was pitch black, I could still find them.

The cardboard box was right where I left it. I picked it up and set it down under the small window in the corner. The fading light coming in was dim and hazy, but there was still enough to see.

I lifted the top and looked at the first photograph. It was the one of me and Dad and the new sandbox he built. I was wearing baggy overalls and holding a hoe. I was practicing to be a farmer.

Tears started to fill my eyes. I didn't want them to. But I guess they'd been building up for quite a while. A second later I started to sniff. That did it. Once the sniffing starts, I'm a goner.

I buried my face in the sleeve of my sweatshirt. Then it all sort of came pouring out at once. I started sobbing and I couldn't stop.

I tried to keep the noise down, but it wasn't easy. Sobbing is like an explosion. All of your emotions erupt like a volcano and everything on your face starts running all at once. The first couple of minutes are the noisiest. But even after that, stuff keeps running. It's a lot to ask a sweatshirt to sop up, if you want to know the truth.

"You okay?"

The voice came out of nowhere. It took me by surprise. Startled, I looked up.

It was Ben! Oh, geez, not now! How had he gotten up the stairs without me hearing?

Instinctively I ducked back into the safety of my soggy sweatshirt. Crying isn't something that I like to do in front of people; I don't care how normal it's supposed to be.

Ben started coming closer. As I heard his footsteps I drew my arms tighter around my hidden face. Somehow I forced myself to stop the tears.

He stood there a moment before sitting down next to me. When he did, our arms touched.

I pulled away.

I was still making quiet snuffling noises by then, but I was pretty much under control. I kept my head down, though. I felt uncomfortable as anything.

Nervously I shifted my feet. What should I do? What should I say? Did he know? Should I confess?

I rolled my eyes. Confess? Yeah, sure . . . right, Charlie.

Oh, by the way, Ben, I made Thomas fall off the

roof and break his collarbone. He's keeping it a secret so I'll like him.

I felt more tears well up in my eyes. I was going to start crying again. I just couldn't find a way out.

Without saying a word, Ben reached out for me. I felt his arm around me, and I buried my face in his shoulder. I didn't even think about it.

We stayed like that until the crying stopped again. It wasn't the noisy kind this time. Just the quiet, muffled sniffling you do when you're finishing up.

Through it all, Ben didn't say a word. Except for my sniffling and a little gulping, the two of us remained silent. The silence wasn't awkward, though. Not like the strained silences we'd had on our trip to Lake Murky.

When I was finished, I lifted my face off his shoulder and wiped my eyes. Ben gave me one last pat and removed his arm. No sense overdoing the hugging stuff. Not when neither one of us was used to it.

I couldn't think of anything to say. I guess Ben couldn't either. The awkwardness was coming between us again. You could almost feel it start to separate us.

I couldn't stand it this time. Maybe it was the guilt. Or maybe I just felt closer to Ben than I had before.

"Thomas fell off the roof," I blurted out suddenly. "I was out there and he reached for me and I pulled away and he fell."

I turned and looked him in the eye. "He did, Ben. I didn't push him. I thought maybe I did at first, but I didn't. I wouldn't have done that. I know I wouldn't have."

Ben took his hand and brushed the hair back from my forehead. Then he looked at me and slowly nodded.

I waited for more, but it never came. He believed me, though. I could see in his eyes that he believed me.

We sat there another couple of minutes before Ben suddenly reached across my lap and picked up the photo of Dad and me and the sandbox. It was lying face down next to my leg. He turned it over and smiled.

The smile turned into a chuckle.

"Great picture," he said, laughing softly. "That hoe was twice as big as you were."

I sniffed and nodded.

He reached out and pulled the cardboard box of photos closer.

"Would you mind if I looked through the rest of these?" he asked, already digging into the carton.

I felt myself tensing up again. There was something about Ben looking into my box of pictures that felt wrong. I mean, the sandbox picture wasn't really that personal. But to look through the whole box—I don't know—it was almost like he was invading my family's privacy or something.

I was still thinking it over when I heard Ben take a deep breath.

"Susan used to take a lot of pictures," he said almost in a whisper.

It was the first time he'd ever mentioned his wife's name. Susan.

Ben didn't get weepy or anything. He just stared into space a second and then quickly reached into the box again. How could I say no after that?

The next picture was the most recent one that Mom and Dad and I had taken together. It was taken in a studio, the kind where the photographer gives you a choice of fake backgrounds to stand in front of.

I cleared my throat. "Those aren't really the Alps," I told Ben. "It's just a picture of Alps."

I wasn't planning to explain every photograph. I just didn't want him asking me a bunch of questions about Switzerland, that's all.

The next picture was taken during one of our first family vacations.

Ben raised his eyebrows. "Disney World?"

"Land," I corrected.

He pointed at me in the picture and smiled. "Thomas has one of those Donald Duck hats."

My face turned red. I've never really forgiven my parents for buying me that hat. I know I begged, but they should have been stronger.

After another second or two, Ben dug deeper into the carton. I swallowed hard. Now we were getting to the personal stuff. My heart began to beat faster. I was almost positive which picture was next.

Maybe I should have warned Ben it was coming.

"Their wedding picture," I blurted loudly.

Ben was surprised. You could see it in his eyes. The glass was smudged and dirty with fingerprints from all the times I'd held it. But he lowered it to his lap and stared through the smudges.

It was one of those pictures that you imagine seeing at the end of fairy tales. My mother was in this beautiful white gown and Dad was wearing one of those suits with a sash around the middle. They were standing in front of the altar in the church, kissing.

See? I wanted to yell. They really *did* love each other once!

I didn't, though. I just sat there with my heart still pounding like crazy while Ben stared down at the picture. It took him a long time, too. I didn't have a watch or anything, but it was definitely a while.

Finally he took a big deep breath and turned to me. Then he smiled this really sad smile.

"It's really been hard on you, hasn't it?" he asked me softly.

I didn't answer.

"I'm sorry," he whispered. "I wish I could have made things easier for you. I just didn't know how."

He put his arm around my shoulders again and held me.

I didn't pull away.

(twelve)

THOMAS GOT to take his sling off a few weeks ago. You can tell that he misses the attention it brought him. The other day he made a sling out of an old towel and wore it to dinner. He asked Lydia to cut his meat loaf. Ben told him to go upstairs until he could act normal.

I guess you could say the two of us are making progress. Thomas and me, I mean. The last time Martin came over to play Monopoly, he started making the top hat and the iron dance with each other.

"Stop it, Thomas," I ordered.

He ignored me.

"I mean it. Put them down."

He continued to dance them around the board. I had no choice.

"Okay, Thomas. That's it. If you don't stop, I'm going to make the hand come out of the closet and kill you."

Thomas isn't as worried about the hand as he used to be. He put his mouth on his arm and started making bathroom noises. He seemed to think this was really hilarious. He was still laughing when I dragged him into the hall and locked him out of the room.

Martin was very impressed. He said as soon as we get a little more violent, we'll be practically normal.

I don't want to make everything sound okay, because it's not. This isn't one of those "they lived happily ever after" endings. I don't believe in those anymore.

Lydia still hogs the phone like crazy. She sits there for hours saying absolutely nothing of interest. I'm serious. I've had better conversations with a Mattel SEE 'N SAY.

Also, she still locks herself in the bathroom. These days I'm not as nice about it as I used to be. If I want to get in there, I just pound on the door and start screaming, "I gotta go! I gotta go!" When it comes to going to the bathroom, I have no pride.

The two of us don't fight exactly. Mostly we just make fun of each other. Like the other night when I took off my tennis shoes, she held her nose.

"P.U.! What died?"

"Whoops, sorry," I apologized. "I almost forgot. Big noses are more sensitive than normal ones."

"There's nothing wrong with my nose," she snapped defensively.

"I didn't say there was, Lydia. Noses like yours come in very handy. If we ever have a fire, you can spray it out."

"Daaa-aad!" she screamed.

When Lydia tattles, she makes *dad* into two syllables.

Speaking of dads, mine took me to the zoo for the hundredth time last weekend. We don't look at the animals anymore. Mostly we just have a picnic lunch and talk and stuff.

My father told me that he'd noticed a difference in me lately.

"You don't seem to be as angry as you used to be," he commented. "What d'you think? You think that maybe you're finally starting to adjust to your new situation?"

"No!" I retorted quickly. "I'm not adjusting.

mean I'm adjusting."

I hate it when parents think you're adjusting. It takes the guilt off of them or something.

I'll tell you one person who's finally started to change, though, and that's my mother. I'm serious. She's finally beginning to treat Thomas the way she should have treated him all along. The other day he called her a "giant poopy" and she marched him right up to our room and made him stay there all day.

Thomas still wasn't speaking to her at dinner. Even though we were having hamburgers, he refused to eat.

I could hardly keep from laughing. It was great seeing someone else in trouble for a change. Just to be annoying, I stuffed a giant bite of cheeseburger into my mouth and grinned at Thomas with my mouth opened. Ben said for me to get down from the table until I could eat like a human being.

Speaking of Thomas, he turned six last week. I gave him my globe. No big deal. I just slapped on a bow and handed it to him during the ice cream and cake.

His eyes lit up like you wouldn't believe. "Mine? Is this for me? I get to have your world?"

I just shrugged. It's not like it cost me anything. And besides, I already know what the world looks like. It's round and it's bumpy and it spins.

But mostly it changes. Volcanoes blow up and the seasons go from winter to summer and every day turns into night. And people get divorced and then they get married again and the next thing you know, you're sharing your bedroom. And sometimes you're angry and sometimes you're sad, and sometimes you're so confused, you don't know what you are.

And they say that time fixes everything, but it doesn't. Not everything. Time can't change what's already happened. It can only help you accept it a little easier, that's all.

And even if some of the anger starts to go away after a while, you don't have to run around telling your parents how much better you're feeling.

And you don't have to eat fiber cereal either.

Oh, yeah, and you don't have to keep your memories in a box in the attic. You can bring them down and put them on your dresser if you want to.

You can.

Ben helped.

BARBARA PARK is one of today's funniest, most popular writers for children. Her novels, including *The Kid in the Red Jacket, Operation: Dump the Chump*, and *Almost Starring Skinnybones,* continue to win just about every award given by children.

Ms. Park holds a B.S. in education from the University of Alabama. She lives outside of Phoenix with her husband and two sons.

Don't Make Me Smile
by Barbara Park

The way Charlie Hickle sees it, there's no reason to smile. His parents are getting a divorce, and there doesn't seem to be anything he can do about it. Not that Charlie doesn't try. He does everything he can think of to convince his parents that he'll go nuts if they get a divorce. He threatens to spend the rest of his life in a tree. He refuses to eat his mother's cooking. He causes trouble in school and makes rude comments about his father's new apartment. With a little help from a new friend, though, Charlie finally starts to accept the inevitable changes in his life—but not until he makes a hilarious last-ditch effort to get his parents back together.

"Funny and touching—a good read."
—*Children's Book Review Service*

"The author does make you smile, proving that there is still room for one more middle-grade problem novel on divorce."
—*Booklist*

BULLSEYE BOOKS PUBLISHED BY ALFRED A. KNOPF